JUNGL
in Slippery Places

⑥

JUNGLE DOCTOR in
Slippery Places

Paul White

CF4·K

Jungle Doctor in Slippery Places, ISBN 978-1-84550-298-0
© Copyright 1988 Paul White
First published in 1973 by African Christian Press as
'Yakobo in Slippery Places'
Revised edition 1988

Published in 2007 by Christian Focus Publications,
Geanies House, Fearn, Tain, Ross-shire,
IV20 1TW, Scotland, U.K.
www.christianfocus.com
Paul White Productions, 4/1-5 Busaco Road,
Marsfield, NSW 2122, Australia.
Cover design by Danie van Straaten.
Cover illustrations by Craig Howarth.
Interior illustrations by Graham Wade.
Printed and bound in Denmark
by Nørhaven Paperback A/S

Since the Jungle Doctor books were first published there have been a number of Jungle Doctors working in Mvumi Hospital, Tanzania, East Africa - some Australian, some British, a West Indian and a number of East African Jungle Doctors to name but a few. This story introduces one of these African doctors, Dr. Daudi Matama.

African words are used throughout the book, but explained at least once within the text. A glossary of the more important words is included at the front along with a key character index.

CONTENTS

Fact Files 6-11

1 Unwelcome Patient............................... 13

2 Area Commissioner................................19

3 Easy Money... 25

4 Snakes for Sale.....................................33

5 Yakobo Tastes Success......................... 41

6 Punda and Pili Pili................................49

7 Weaver Birds...55

8 In The Cooking Pot............................... 65

9 Complications.......................................71

10 Yakobo Sinks Deeper.......................... 77

11 Thugs.. 87

12 Man or Bird? 99

13 Nightmare...109

14 Eaten by Ants 115

15 Potful of Flame 127

16 Out of the Swamp...............................139

Sample Chapter....................................150-158

Fact File: Paul White

Born in 1910 in Bowral, New South Wales, Australia, Paul had Africa in his blood for as long as he could remember. His father captured his imagination with stories of his experiences in the Boer War which left an indelible impression. His father died of meningitis in army camp in 1915 and he was left an only child without his father at five years of age. He inherited his father's storytelling gift along with a mischievous sense of humour.

He committed his life to Christ as a sixteen-year-old school-boy and studied medicine as the next step towards missionary work in Africa. Paul and his wife, Mary, left Sydney, with their small son, David, for Tanganyika in 1938. He always thought of this as his life's work but Mary's severe illness forced their early return to Sydney in 1941. Their daughter, Rosemary, was born while they were overseas.

Within weeks of landing in Sydney Paul was invited to begin a weekly radio broadcast which spread throughout Australia as the Jungle Doctor Broadcasts - the last of these was aired in 1985. The weekly scripts for these programmes became the raw material for the Jungle Doctor hospital stories - a series of twenty books.

Paul always said he preferred life to be a 'mixed grill' and so it was: writing, working as a Rheumatologist, public speaking, involvement with many Christian organisations, adapting the fable stories into multiple forms (comic books, audio cassettes, filmstrips), radio and television, and sharing his love of birds with others by producing bird song cassettes - and much more…

The books in part or whole have been translated into 107 languages.

Paul saw that although his plan to work in Africa for life was turned on its head, in God's better planning he was able to reach more people by coming home than by staying. It was a great joy to meet people over the years who told him they were on their way overseas to work in mission because of the books.

Paul's wife, Mary, died after a long illness in 1970. He married Ruth and they had the joy of working together on many new projects. He died in 1992 but the stories and fables continue to attract an enthusiastic readership of all ages.

Fact file: Tanzania

The Jungle Doctor books are based on Paul White's missionary experiences in Tanzania. Today many countries in Africa have gained their independence. This has resulted in a series of name changes. Tanganyika is one such country that has now changed its name to Tanzania.

The name Tanganyika is no longer used formally for the territory. Instead the name Tanganyika is used almost exclusively to mean the lake.

During World War I what was then Tanganyika came under British military rule. On December 9, 1961 it became independent. In 1964, it joined with the islands of Zanzibar to form the United Republic of Tanganyika and Zanzibar, changed later in the year to the United Republic of Tanzania.

It is not only its name that has changed, this area of Africa has gone through many changes since the Jungle Doctor books were first written. Africa itself has changed. Many of the same diseases raise their heads, but treatments have advanced. However new diseases come to take their place and the work goes on.

Missions throughout Africa are often now run by African Christians and not solely by foreign nationals. There are still the same problems to overcome however. The message of the gospel thankfully never changes and brings hope to those who listen and obey. *The Jungle Doctor* books are about this work to bring health and wellbeing to Africa as well as the good news of Jesus Christ and salvation.

Fact File: Characters

Let's find out a bit about the people in the story before we start. Bwana is the Chief Doctor at the hospital and the key character. He's the one who is often telling the stories as they happen - and is also known as The Jungle Doctor. Daudi is his deputee or assistant. There are a lot of others working at the hospital too such as Wendwa and Yakobo. There are other characters as well. Take a moment or two now to familiarise yourself with their names.

Baruti - the hunter

Doctor Daudi Matama: Doctor in charge at Mvumi hospital

Dolla - the thief who sets Yakobo off on the wrong track

Iyubu - Pakistani shopkeeper

Mboga - member of the hospital staff

Nelson Kolongo - the Area Commissioner

Noha - a Christian from the village of Furahi

Sergeant Mboto - Policeman

Tembo - a young boy who helps Baruti on safari

Wendwa - nurse at hospital

Winston Churchill Lugu - a troublemaker along with Dolla

Yakobo - Senior Male Nurse (Bwana Jacob)

Yonah Nhuti - the game scout

Fact File: Words

Askari - Police officers

Bwana - a term of respect

Fez - a hat

Hatari - Danger

Hodi - May I come in

Lete Pombe - bring beer
Panga - a large knife
Pole - Gently

EXPRESSIONS THAT ADD EMPHASIS:
Eeeeh; Eheh; Heeeh; Hongo; Kah; Koh; Kumbe; Yoh.

TANZANIAN LANGUAGES:
Swahili (main language)
Chigogo (one of the 150 tribal languages)

Fact File: Hunting

In the past wild animals throughout Africa were hunted and transported live to zoos and safaris across the world. This gave an extra source of income to the hunters and trackers in the local population. When the animals were transported live it also meant that people in other countries could become more knowledgable of these amazing species. Nowadays zoos and safaris have much more expertise about the animals in their care and breeding programmes within these animal sanctuaries has reduced the need to capture from the wild. Those species that are now endangered due to over hunting and poaching cling to survival through captive breeding programmes such as these. The wildlife of Africa is still a source of much needed income to rural communities throughout the continent. Tourists come from all over the world in order to capture wild animals on film rather than in cages.

1
Unwelcome Patient

'That man Dolla is with us again,' said Doctor Daudi Matama.

Mboga laughed. 'Truly, his head is of bone. He dived through the window of the train because he thought he saw a policeman. I saw it happen. His arms held tightly to a steel box and his head struck a large stone with a heavy thump.'

'Did you use the wisdom you are taught here?'

'That and more,' chuckled Mboga. 'Is he not here in the men's ward, sewn up, bandaged, treated for shock and doing as well as can be expected? But, Dr Daudi, you should have seen his clothes – lovely colours. They will make Yakobo's eyes stick out with jealousy.'

In the ward the young doctor examined the injured man. He turned to Yakobo, the hospital's senior male nurse. 'Dolla needs rest and quiet. Call me if his pulse rate changes.'

As he went through the door the doctor was

remembering, 'When Dolla and that trickster Lugu were in here a year ago a change started to come over Yakobo. I only hope Dolla's present visit doesn't make things worse.'

Yakobo counted the unconscious man's pulse and noted it on his chart. He picked up the double-locked steel box, put it in a cupboard and packed Dolla's folded clothing neatly on top of it. He sighed.

From the far end of the ward a quavering voice demanded, 'Give me medicines for the snake within me.' Yakobo grunted. A small boy chose that moment to be violently sick. Yakobo groaned aloud.

Glancing at the clock he saw it was time to take Dolla's pulse again. His hand had barely touched the bandaged wrist when Dolla's one visible eye opened. There was a gleam in it.

Huskily the sick man spoke. 'There is a key in my pocket. Open the steel box and take out a parcel and a transistor radio. Hide that parcel safely and the radio is yours.'

Yakobo whispered urgently, 'Keep your voice down. Mboga is here and his ears are large.'

'So is his mouth,' hissed Dolla. 'This matter must be kept secret.'

Mboga strolled up. 'How's our tough friend?'

Yakobo shook his head, put his hand on Mboga's shoulder and tiptoed with him to the door. 'We must keep him quiet and give complete rest. Please go and tell Dr Daudi that the pulse is slower and temperature normal.'

Mboga was no sooner out of sight than Yakobo

moved to the cupboard, unlocked the box and pushed two packages up his shirt.

At midday the doctor came to the ward. Dolla was propped up, muttering and breathing fast. 'Hold him forward, Yakobo. I want to listen to his chest.' After a minute Dr Daudi Matama took his stethoscope from his ears. 'It's penicillin for him, or he'll have pneumonia on top of his head injuries.'

Yakobo nodded, went to the medicine cupboard and returned with a syringe and penicillin. He rolled up Dolla's sleeve and said in a low voice, 'Your parcel is fixed firmly under the ward table with sticking plaster. No one ever looks under there.'

'OK,' muttered Dolla.

Yakobo injected expertly.

Again Dolla's eye opened. 'You do that well. I've had many injections but none as good as that.'

Yakobo felt a warm glow inside him.

Dolla's voice came again, 'Why work here for wages that only whisper in your pocket when you could be rich and buy anything you want?'

Yakobo shrugged. 'I have told you before, there is much interest and satisfaction in the work of the hospital.'

Dolla sneered. 'You can't eat, drink or wear satisfaction and interest. Do you enjoy listening to the complaining voices of the sick or doing work that is not food for the nose? What joy you must get out of giving medicines and making beds! What satisfaction there must be in working at night when you might be sleeping or better still be in the town having fun!'

The male nurse put down the syringe. 'What are you up to, Dolla? Does it please you to disturb my mind and bring unsettling thoughts into my head?'

There was disgust in Dolla's voice. 'Disturb! Unsettle! Are you a complete fool? Doesn't your mind protest when you hear voices that order, Yakobo do this, Yakobo do that, Yakobo come here, Yakobo go there? Open your eyes, man! For merely hiding a packet you've become the owner of a powerful transistor radio. Can't you see that with enough penicillin and the skill you have you could quickly become rich, amazingly rich, in the villages and towns? Many desire medicine for the disease that is spoken of only in whispers.' His voice was high-pitched with excitement. 'There are thousands and thousands of shillings for someone like you with the right people to help him.'

'Yakobo,' called a voice urgently. 'Yakobo.'

'What was I saying?' breathed Dolla. 'If you're fool enough to keep on living this way, it's your affair.'

Yakobo turned away sharply. As he hurried down the ward he stumbled, grabbed at the syringe and missed. Mboga stood in the doorway and laughed. 'There is no joy in broken syringes. Last week I lost two shillings from my wages for doing that.'

Kicking the glass under a bed, Yakobo walked out

of the ward. He glanced at the marking on the sleeve of his tunic and thought, 'After seven years' service, because I do not make trouble I'm pushed about and ordered to do this and that like a first-year trainee.'

He passed a window. Dr Matama's voice called. 'Yakobo, don't forget you have those blood specimens to examine.'

With difficulty he replied quietly, 'Yes, doctor.' His head seemed to throb with anger as he muttered under his breath, 'Dolla was right. I've something better to do than work with a microscope. I'll listen to the world on that transistor and I'll tune in to any station I want.'

Then he saw a bunch of keys in the storeroom door. One of these he knew would open the dispensary. There were riches for him in that dispensary with its bottles of penicillin and syringes and needles. He made sure no one was looking, then in a few seconds the key was off the bunch and in his pocket.

2

Area Commissioner

At midday Nelson Kolongo ate a hasty lunch. He placed two reports in his briefcase and stepped briskly into the police jeep. A minute later he and a tall sergeant were moving fast along the road that led south from the East African town of Mabwe. The road wound between small hills covered with boulders and then emerged into rolling thornbush country.

After an hour's driving, Nelson Kolongo looked up from the report he was trying to read and smiled. 'This is my home country, Sergeant. I was born beyond those baobab trees and I have been a patient in that hospital more than once.'

Daudi Matama shaded his eyes. 'That looks like a jeep and our old friend, Nelson Kolongo. Wendwa, it is a hot day. If it is the Area Commissioner, he will have a thirst.'

The nurse replied promptly, 'I shall use the large teapot. He is a man of importance.'

'Truly,' said Daudi, 'no one would have thought when a boy came to this hospital years ago with an arrow wound in his eye that today he would be the leading man in this part of the country.'

Wendwa smiled. 'I have heard the story. The work of the hospital is good. It is hard these days to tell which eye is real and which is of glass.'

The jeep pulled up outside the hospital. The doctor hurried to the gate.

'What is the news, Bwana A.C.?'

'The news is good, Bwana Doctor.'

'Excellent. Come and have a cup of tea.'

'Thank you. But Sergeant Mboto has immediate work to do. There has been a theft of two thousand shillings and we suspect a man called Dolla. I believe he is here.'

Daudi Matama nodded. 'The man who jumped off a train and disappeared?'

The policeman saluted. 'True, Bwana. Have you any objection to our interviewing him and searching his effects?'

'He has concussion. Go gently. You will have some difficulty with his steel box.'

'Search that box, Sergeant,' ordered the A.C., 'and report to me in half an hour.'

The doctor picked up the teapot. 'Thank you.' The Area Commissioner drank thirstily. 'Daudi, you know the swamp country at the foot of the Great Rift Wall? Now, I have the feeling that this rather foul spot could be turned into a useful piece of fertile land and grow enough rice to feed the people for a hundred kilometres around. What's more, I think that the job could be done cheaply using materials available on the spot. This could be a pattern to sharpen people's minds to do similar things in other parts of Africa.'

Daudi Matama nodded. 'I think you're right. I did a medical safari through the Malenga country a year ago. It's a place of millions of flies and thousands of millions of mosquitoes and therefore there is much eye disease and still more malaria. It's an interesting place though. But whatever is done will need most careful planning.'

'I agree,' said the A.C. 'And everybody knows that there are strange goings-on in that part of the country – traffic in ivory, growing and selling marijuana, and other dangerous drugs.' He stopped for breath. 'The first step would be to find some observant person doing ordinary work who could walk right through the country.'

Dr Daudi sat in deep thought and then jumped to his feet. 'Baruti, who used to work with the Game Scout, is the man you want. He is a well-known snake catcher. He could be catching snakes and at the same time spying out the land.'

Kolongo put down his cup. 'Splendid. And these days there are those in Mabwe who will buy reptiles and young animals for overseas zoos. There is an airstrip at the side of the swamp. When we're ready we must move fast.'

The doctor nodded and the A.C. continued rapidly, 'Conditions in Africa are different these days. The population grows fast and feeding our people well is an urgent need.'

Dr. Matama nodded again. 'I like the government's policy of encouraging the people to realise their responsibilities and to become self-reliant. It would be useful if we could drain off the water, store it and re-use it for irrigation.'

The A.C. broke in, 'For a place without rain for eight consecutive months each year it would be a great help!'

Daudi Matama was enthusiastic. 'We'd be killing two birds with one stone.'

Kolongo chuckled. 'Killing birds does come into this. There could be a plague of weaver birds. In certain places in East Africa there are myriads of them. They threaten to eat most of this year's harvest.'

The police sergeant stood at attention near the door. 'Reporting box and clothing of suspect Dolla examined. No stolen articles found. Nine shillings in cash. Clothes are new and expensive.'

The A.C. nodded. 'Thank you, Sergeant. Doctor Matama, you must excuse me if I move on. There is much to be done.'

The jeep's engine roared and Nelson Kolongo waved farewell. Two minutes later he ordered his driver, 'Stop at the house near the tall baobab tree.'

He jumped to the ground and greeted Baruti. They sat in the shade while the A.C. repeated enthusiastically the plans he had for the swamp country.

Baruti listened carefully and from time to time asked a question. Then he stood up. 'I agree with your words and will travel the Malenga country with my eyes and ears open. But, I ask that the boy, Tembo, who has recovered from the great cough, may travel with me. He would help me and I can help him. He has good wisdom and will quickly understand your plans. After all there was a boy once who came to this hospital with an eye injury...'

The A.C. smiled musingly. 'Wait till you hear from me and then go on the safari.'

He shook hands, called 'goodbye' and the jeep swung around and drove away rapidly.

3
Easy Money

Early that evening Mboga strolled through the hospital. He stopped outside Yakobo's room.

'May I come in?' he called.

No answer. He turned the knob. The door was locked.

Inside, a perspiring young man pushed a sizeable radio under a pile of shirts. As he threw a blanket over his half-packed suitcase he shouted, 'Wait a minute, can't you!'

When he opened the door Mboga strolled in, gazed around and asked, 'What's happening? Why are you…?'

Yakobo pushed him back through the door. 'What do you want? Can't you see I'm busy?'

Mboga rolled his eyes. 'Keep calm. I came to bring you news. The A.C. turned up after you went off duty and with him came police. It was exciting. They undid Dolla's box and went through his clothes but found nothing. You should have seen that sergeant's face. He expected to find bags of money.'

'I don't care what they found,' snapped Yakobo. 'Clear out.'

'Behold,' grinned Mboga, 'I diagnose stomach trouble. What you need is the white medicine for insides that rumble and heads that have no joy in them.'

The door slammed in his face and the lock clicked shut. Mboga walked away slowly and thoughtfully.

Inside, Yakobo strode across the room muttering angrily. He bumped into a pile of books. They tumbled about his feet. From one book slid a folded sheet of cardboard on which was written in large letters, 'If sinners entice you, don't you consent.'

Yakobo picked up the cardboard, looked at his Bible which was lying cover downwards on the floor, and pushed it under the bed with his foot. He read again what he had written months before. He had used it to give a talk to the men in the ward. He tore the cardboard into pieces and put them in his pocket, ignoring deliberately the odd feeling in the pit of his stomach as he finished packing.

He groped in his pocket for the charm that he had bought from the medicine-man a month before and clutched it tightly in his hand with the keys that he had stolen. He waited till the hospital was quiet, then crept through his door. His plans went smoothly. There was no one to notice a darkly clad figure walking away carrying a suitcase in one hand and bulky parcel in the other, which contained, among other things, half the hospital's stock of penicillin.

Always keeping in the shadow, he chose a seldom used path which went steeply downhill. Gradually the lights of the hospital disappeared. He grunted with relief. Before anyone realised he had gone he would be far away.

In the darkness, he smiled with satisfaction. It really had been easy. Dolla was right. You had only to make your plans and… Hooked thorns tore into his leg. He gasped, bent down to free himself and dropped his torch. Again thorns stabbed at him as he groped in the gloom. When he pressed the switch no light came.

He muttered in disgust. 'Now I must walk in darkness.' Words from his memory flooded his head: 'Men prefer darkness to light because their deeds are evil.'

Yakobo cursed his unusual ability to remember words. He limped on into the night.

After a while agreeable thoughts started to move again into his mind. He thought of those to whom he owed money and grinned. Walking on downhill, he stopped abruptly when he thought he heard footsteps behind him. Hardly daring to breathe he stood absolutely still in deep shadow. Nothing happened.

After a time he moved on again. He had always wanted to travel. If some of the towns and villages were now closed to him he would go further afield. He could go to Nairobi or to Dar-es-Salaam at the coast.

There was a rustling in the undergrowth behind him. He dropped his suitcase and the box of penicillin, picked up a large stone and held it above his head. His skin started to creep. The eerie laughter of a hyaena sounded ominous at his back. Yakobo hurled the stone and there was silence. Picking up his suitcase and box again, he hurried on into the night. The path wound through tall, thorn-covered acacia trees.

His load seemed heavier but he dared not stop. The moon made the shadows appear long and full of threats. The luminous dial of his watch told him it was an hour after midnight. He struggled on until he was too tired to go any further. He slumped down on a gnarled tree root, put his head on the penicillin box and fell into a troubled sleep.

Yakobo woke with a start. Two yellow eyes were coming at him through the greyness of dawn. He struggled to his feet. With a mixture of anger and relief he saw the headlights of a lorry moving down the road. He stood still and watched the countryside emerge rapidly out of the night.

Not far away was the village of Magoli – a cluster of mud-brick shops sheltered by umbrella trees. He had friends there, in particular Iyubu, a plump Pakistani shopkeeper.

He went to the shop. After the usual greetings, Iyubu said, 'It is a matter of joy to see you, Bwana Yakobo. I and three others plan to visit the hospital for injections. Perhaps you can help us here. Have you medicine with you?'

Yakobo nodded. The Pakistani came close and said in low tones, 'It is not always easy at the hospital. We know the injections we want but they listen to our chests, look down our throats, or take a drop of our blood. Then they say, "Ah yes, we have the treatment for you." But what we want is the injection that has great strength. Have you this one with you?'

Yakobo stifled a yawn and nodded again.

'Good. It will be to your profit to help us. Come.'

They walked to a room at the back of the shop. Dramatically Iyubu took down a parcel wrapped in plastic.

'This will delight your eyes. It is a bed but it folds up like a blanket. This is a valve. Blow through it and it fills with air like a tyre – most comfortable and convenient. Only those who know their way about have this kind of thing.'

Yakobo unwound the air bed and inflated it. He lay on it and was amazed how comfortable he felt. Pushing the section for the pillow up and down with his thumb he said, 'I will accept this, but I will also need to rest here until later today.'

In the late morning a bus pulled up. A smart-looking man in a red fez walked briskly into Iyubu's shop.

'May I speak to Bwana Yakobo from the hospital? It is a matter of importance and urgency.'

The voice woke Yakobo, who stumbled to his feet in alarm. The man with the red fez was at the door in a second.

'Bwana Yakobo, well met. What a happy occasion! I am Winston Churchill Lugu. You remember me? You treated me when I was in hospital last year. I've heard your news. We will work together admirably, I am sure, for there is money in medicine.'

Yakobo smiled. 'You speak truly. See this modern-type bed? It is mine for giving just four injections.'

Lugu murmured, 'Oh, no! You gave four injections to four men and all you received in payment was that second-hand air bed? My unfortunate friend! Nothing is more certain than that many shillings, rightly yours, now rattle in the pocket of that rascal Iyubu.' He sighed. 'You have more penicillin with you?' His roving eye took in the large cardboard box and the suitcase. 'I see you have. Let us work together. Fifty-fifty. The place to find real profit is not here under the hospital's nose but at Nungho in the middle of the swamp – a village of real opportunity that.'

'How did you know where to find me?' demanded Yakobo.

'Simple. You leave the hospital rather suddenly, and by night. Now it's fourteen kilometres to the main road which can take you anywhere and it's thirty kilometres over the hill to Mabwe. You, a man of intelligence, would choose the shorter route.' Lugu chuckled. 'Small conversation with that unwise individual, Dolla, and open ears to the talk of the hospital and it was obvious. Now, to business. You give the injections. I find the patients and discuss the financial side.'

Lugu sprang to his feet, pushed Yakobo behind a curtain and moved briskly to the door. From a safari-bodied car stepped a young man, dressed in Western fashion. He walked through the door to be met with a beaming smile.

'Good morning, Mr Mpala. My name is Lugu. Will you join me in a cup of tea?'

'I have little time. I am on my way to the hospital.' Mr Mpala attempted to push his way past.

Lugu chuckled. 'Then the news I heard is true?'

The man opposite him clenched his fist.

Lugu stepped back and held up his hands. 'Peace. Let us think with calm minds.'

Yakobo listened with his mouth wide open. The blue-suited man muttered, 'Speak more softly.'

Lugu shrugged. 'Let me put you into the picture. This disease is no joke. It is dangerous. There are pills to treat it, but these cost money and work slowly. Also, quite frankly, I doubt their usefulness. Then, there is the everyday injection for which the price is a goat.'

'Do I have goats in my motor car?'

Lugu laughed. 'I want to give you special news. I can obtain and supply, here and now, an expert to give you the special medicine that those at the hospital reserve for themselves. It's expensive, but…'

'How much is this medicine?'

'Thirty shillings, exactly,' replied Lugu.'

'I'll give fifteen.'

'Winston Churchill Lugu is not in the habit of running auction sales. I'm doing you a great favour as it is.'

Behind the curtain Yakobo listened. He thought, 'So this is the way it's done?' Already he had learned a great deal.

Later, when he was putting away his syringe, Lugu handed him three five shilling notes and smiled. 'Money for nothing, you agree?' His voice changed. 'But, remember, if you do not co-operate, my friend, Mr Kolongo will be interested to hear of your whereabouts. So, watch your step.'

Outside a jeep skidded to a stop. Yakobo dived behind a high pile of bagged beans.

In the entrance to the shop appeared a police sergeant with a document in his hand. In a deep voice he announced, 'Winston Churchill Lugu, I am arresting you on a charge of fraud.'

4
Snakes for Sale

Twelve kilometres to the east, Baruti, the snake catcher, came to the door of Daudi Matama's house and said, 'May I come in?'

'Welcome,' came the reply.

'What is the news of Yakobo?'

'There is no sign of him. He has disappeared with much penicillin, syringes and a number of needles.'

The doctor sighed and pointed to a picture of Jesus as the Light of the world. 'These days many in good jobs, and those who seek good jobs, do not believe what that picture tells. They say that the light of the world is not Jesus Christ but the shilling.'

'Is that what has happened to Yakobo?'

'I think so. He has stolen medicines and equipment and he'll start a black market in penicillin injections. For many days his thoughts have been fixed on the idea of becoming rich quickly, and now Dolla appears again and this happens.'

Baruti shook his head. 'If only Yakobo had used the preventive medicine of a pair of closed ears to this temptation it would have saved him much trouble and much sadness. No good will come to him out of this thing.'

'Truly. His trouble started when he ceased to feed his soul and left his Bible on the shelf with the other books he didn't read.'

They sat in silence for some minutes until Baruti spoke. 'What we want is an eagle's-eye view of the Malenga country. Later we can look it over piece by piece with the watchfulness of a fox. If we are to drain the swamp this will be necessary.'

'The Missionary Aviation Fellowship pilot knows exactly what to do.'

'This is wisdom,' nodded Baruti. 'But can I take Tembo too?'

'It is already arranged,' rejoined Daudi with satisfaction.

Baruti's deep voice boomed out, 'Splendid. My name means *dynamite* and his means *elephant*. Between us we'll have action.'

Two weeks later, an hour after sun-up, the M.A.F. plane landed on the hospital airstrip. Baruti and Tembo hurried down the path through the millet gardens. Over Baruti's shoulder was a basket with his spear threaded through the handles. Tembo importantly carried a large canvas bag.

They shook hands with the pilot who asked, 'You haven't anything dangerous in your loads?'

'Nothing, Bwana. Nothing except a somewhat large cobra here in the canvas bag. I caught it only an hour ago.'

The airman stepped back hastily. 'Is it alive?'

'Of that there is no doubt but he's quite safe,' smiled Baruti. 'There is no poison in his fangs, either.'

As he was speaking Dr Matama came striding down the path. 'Greetings,' he called. 'What's the news?'

Two voices in two different languages answered him. The pilot's went on by far the longer and Baruti chuckled, 'Bwana Daudi, he has unease within him because of one cobra.'

The doctor chuckled. 'So would anybody else. Tie the bag with another piece of rope. There would be small joy if the snake got out while you are in the air.'

The airman nodded vigorously and smiled. 'The plan is to fly over the hills there to the north-west. This will bring us right over the Malenga country. Try to picture it all in your mind. It will appear flat from high up but the swamps will be green. Look out for the villages and any special paths that you can see. I will bring the plane down a little if we see anything interesting.'

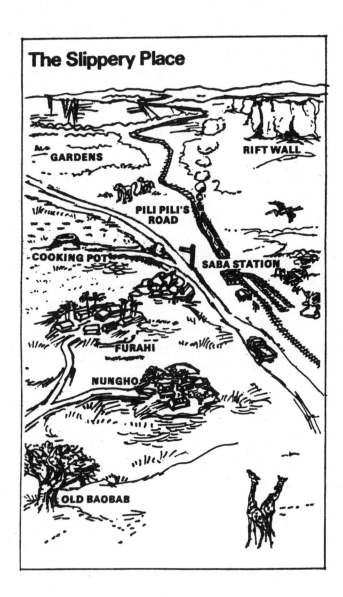

The Slippery Place

GARDENS

RIFT WALL

PILI PILI'S ROAD

COOKING POT

SABA STATION

FURAHI

NUNGHO

OLD BAOBAB

'Those are words of value,' said Baruti. 'Particularly, I want to look down into a place that people fear, called the Cooking Pot of Ghosts. It lies in the middle of the swamp. Above it is cloud that looks like steam. From within it come rumblings and screamings.'

Baruti clambered into the plane. Tembo was close behind him. Placing the bagged snake beside him, Tembo fastened his seat belt and at once began helping Baruti with his.

The pilot went through the routine check of his instruments. The plane moved forward, gathered speed, bumped over a rough patch on the airstrip and was up, climbing steeply. Below was the green of the millet gardens and the deep brown of the sand in the river bed. They flew over the baobabs which seemed to change from enormous trees to squat green toadstools. The aeroplane circled over the hospital. The buildings looked like a drawing on the ground.

Baruti, wide-eyed, saw the plane's shadow cross the river and then become big as they flew over a tall cone-shaped hill topped with lumps of granite. Other hills came and went at a speed that made him gasp.

They heard the pilot's voice loud and clear, 'See those two peaks ahead of us? I'm going between them, then right in front of us will be swamp country.'

The hunter nodded. He and Tembo peered down intently. The airman moved his controls. 'I'll climb and you will be able to see it all at one time, then I will circle and we'll come down low over the tree tops. See?'

Stretched out far to the north were patches of brown and green and straw colour. Baruti could see the far side of the swamp. There was the grey of granite and the dark green of thornbush, huge patches of cactus and, here and there, a clearing and a garden or a village.

Baruti spoke, 'I have seen. It is in my memory. There would be wisdom now in looking into the Cooking Pot.'

The pilot brought the plane down steeply. Baruti and Tembo caught a glimpse of a deep hole with sloping sides and a dark gash at the bottom. For a few seconds they were in a cloud, then came dazzling sunlight showing up a strip of land running deep into the swamp from the main road. It forked to end in two sizeable villages. They flew on for ten minutes.

Automatically the pilot noted the North-South road, took down his microphone and started to speak to the aerodrome. Out of the corner of his eye he could see Baruti deep in thought. The town of Mabwe seemed to rush up at them. They landed smoothly.

A fast-driven jeep came over the tarmac and pulled up near the aircraft. Nelson Kolongo stepped down from it, called a greeting to the pilot and beckoned to Baruti.

'There is little time. Soon we must meet those who buy animals, then you will be driven to the swamp country. Your work there is to catch animals.' A shadow of a smile passed over his face, 'Let these words of hunting be known to everybody, and while you hunt, watch the people. Listen to their words.' When Baruti said nothing he continued, 'See what you think of the soil. You're a man of experience. You will keep in touch with the Game Scout, Nhuti. I will talk to him from time to time on the radio. Instructions from me will come through him. Understand?'

Baruti nodded. 'And I will find out all I can about the swamp.'

'Right,' said Kolongo. 'Here we are.'

He pulled up outside his office and hurried in with Baruti and Tembo. The discussion with the animal dealers was brief and satisfactory.

'They want reptiles and young animals. They must be healthy and uninjured.'

'Have they anything to show us yet?' asked a tall American.

Tembo grinned. 'There is a fine cobra in the bag under the Area Commissioner's chair next to where you are standing!'

5

Yakobo Tastes Success

Yakobo had been extremely careful in his travel to Nungho. His injections were in demand. He had had a most successful two weeks. He had found a satisfactory place to live, with shuttered windows and a thick wooden door with both a lock and a bolt. The sun-dried brick walls were solid and secure. His air-bed was comfortable.

Yakobo heard sounds of an aircraft flying overhead. He looked up. It was the M.A.F. plane. For a moment homesickness overcame him, but the feeling did not last long when he caught a glimpse of himself in his mirror. He straightened his yellow tie. These were the clothes he had dreamed of wearing ever since he'd first met Dolla.

He'd never had as much money as he had at the moment. Shillings certainly grew on the penicillin tree. His new pressure lamp, his powerful transistor radio and a collection of things he'd always wanted stood on top of his cupboard. A twist of the knob of the radio and music from Radio Tanzania filled the room. His foot beat time to the music while his eyes feasted on his shining new bicycle, the portable gramophone and the pile of records.

'*Hodi*,' called a voice. 'Bwana, may I come in?'

Yakobo unlocked the door. 'Bwana, I want an injection.'

Yakobo sat down in a deck chair. 'You have ten shillings?'

'I merely wanted the everyday injection, not the one of great strength.'

Yakobo yawned. 'You have ten shillings?'

'Bwana Yakobo, I have only seven.'

'Return then when you find the other three.'

The man sighed. 'Now there happen to be three more in my other pocket. This is a thing of amazement.'

Yakobo hoisted himself out of the chair, took the money and locked it in the box. The giving of the injection took less than half a minute. He had already given five others that morning. He returned the syringe and the needle to the homemade steriliser and asked some personal questions. 'You will need two more injections.'

'But I have no more shillings.'

Yakobo shrugged. 'The sickness you found for yourself. The pain and misery is yours. The medicine is here that will cure it. If you have no money then bring a goat.'

As he sat comfortably in his deck chair a voice from his memory spoke very clearly: 'Don't lay up treasure on earth where moth and rust consume, where thieves break in and steal. Where your treasure is, that's where your heart will be also.' He felt irritated that words from the Bible kept coming into his mind.

A grin came back to Yakobo's face as he started to think about thieves. He'd never even thought about them till he had met Dolla. He felt complacent, for there were thirty shillings under lock and key in the place where thieves would certainly look. But who would search under the penicillin boxes? They weren't locked up. Everyone could see the tops of the bottles. There was nothing to suggest that underneath, carefully folded, were a thousand shillings in notes. He carried his chair outside and relaxed in the sun.

Baruti and Tembo were not nearly so comfortably seated beside the jeep driver. He whipped the sturdy little machine round corners, skidded in the sand and made it jump like a buck over some large bumps in the road. They came to the beginning of the swamp country.

Putting the jeep into its lowest gear the police driver chuckled. 'Here comes a bridge of small joy.'

It proved to be two huge tree trunks topped by rough-cut, insecurely anchored timber spanning a sluggish, muddy stream. It rattled and rocked as they crossed.

The driver laughed again. 'Those who like real danger go down there.' He pointed to a large flat rock, partly covered by water. 'On this basks a great snake. People say it is twice as long as a giraffe's neck and full of cunning.'

'Stop your machine. We travel from here on foot,' said Baruti.

The driver shrugged, stopped, started again, skidded the jeep in a U-turn and rocketed off the way they had come.

Down on the flat rock Baruti pointed. 'Python was here not long ago. See, Tembo, there is the story in the dust.' The great snake had moved along a path which was marked with paw marks of animals who had come to drink.

In the shade Baruti and Tembo put down their packs, squatted on their heels and prayed that God would help them in what they planned to do. 'Let's go, Tembo,' said Baruti, 'we have work to do. You go first and read the signs.'

The boy's eyes glistened with excitement as he followed without difficulty the track which the snake had left. For two hours they walked through thornbush and palm tree country following the course of the stream. Due west was the deep blue of the Great Rift Wall. South was the row of hills they had flown over earlier in the day. Before them stretched the swamp. Overhead flew a huge flock of birds, wheeling and turning in the air like an enormous flag in a strong breeze. In the thorn trees were scores of weaver birds' nests.

Baruti spat. 'The small birds will destroy these trees.'

Tembo nodded. 'And they will do terrible damage to the crops.'

The python's tracks were blotted out by huge footprints. A large rhino and a small one had passed that way not long before.

The boy chuckled. 'As we flew over, did you notice

44

the great hole in the hillside that looks like that rhino's footprint?'

Baruti nodded. 'Those holes seem to go deep down and have a rim raising their edge above the country round about.'

Directly in front of them was the smaller of the craters. The sun lit up three granite rocks balanced on top of each other that stood high above the rim.

When they reached the boulders the hunter said, 'Tembo, guard my gear and keep out of sight.'

The boy nodded and scrambled into a crevice. He watched Baruti climb to the top of the rocks and stand there. Below him stretched a natural crater a kilometre across. A well-marked path twisted down the slope through stunted thornbush and disappeared into a stand of tall acacia trees. It appeared again on the far side of these, cutting through tall grass and then winding between large boulders.

The high pitched chattering of weaver birds filled the air. Their nests dangled from the limbs of hundreds of umbrella trees. From the far side of these came a grey-haired man running in an irregular zig-zag. He swerved, throwing himself into the tall grass. A huge snake hurled its coils at where the man had been a split second before. He rolled over, bounced back on his feet and moved fast towards the trees.

Baruti scrambled down the boulders and shouted to Tembo, 'Stay where you are!' He knew that pythons come close to their victims, crash them to the ground and then crush them. The hunter was halfway down the path when the reptile struck again. But again the grey-headed man swung aside at the very last moment. He had reached the shelter of the trees and was dodging between their trunks when the snake, moving fast, came up with him. It coiled itself to strike for the third time. Baruti saw its powerful body in the air and then heard a heavy thump. He dashed up and found the man exhausted, but still on his feet, reaching for a stone to finish off the snake which lay like a great heap of rope.

'No!' yelled Baruti. 'Don't! I want it alive.'

'It hit its head on a tree,' panted the man. 'It'll attack again in a minute.'

Baruti pulled off his shirt, ripped out a sleeve, knotted it at the wrist and pulled it over the python's head. He threw the shirt to his companion. 'Tear it into strips.'

He ran across to a patch of tall bamboo and cut a pole as thick as his arm and longer than the snake. With lengths of shirt he tied the python to the pole then stood up wiping sweat from his forehead. 'It's better that way,' he gasped.

The man who had been chased looked up and nodded. 'But for the goodness of God I should be dead by now.'

'True,' agreed Baruti. 'But if you knew the goodness of God that should not worry you.'

A smile spread over the face opposite him. 'These are words of value. My name is Noha. I come from the village of Furahi and am one of those whose Chief is the Bwana Yesu Cristo.'

'This is the thing above all others,' nodded Baruti. 'Today as I set out on my safari I asked him to keep my feet in his paths. I am Baruti from the village where the hospital is. I am collecting snakes to sell to those who choose to have animals of danger in their gardens.'

Noha smiled. 'How are you going to carry this overgrown worm to the people you mention?'

'With your help,' said Baruti, 'we will carry him to the house of Yonah Nhuti, the Game Scout. He has a jeep.'

Noha nodded. 'Let us tie the snake's head and tail securely. There is no joy in being hit by one or the other.'

Carrying the python they walked up the path to the boulders. Tembo greeted Noha politely even as he was jumping up and down with excitement. 'Is he safe? Can he...?'

Baruti's eyes twinkled as he cut off lengths of rope. 'It would be a thing of small charity to give snake the fear that he might fall from this bamboo.'

With the snake secured, Baruti stood on the edge of the crater and looked out over the swamp with its reeds and rushes growing in slimy water. There were trees of various sizes on islands dotted here and there. In the distance was a sweep of deep green. Closer, within the swamp itself, were patches of more vivid hue.

'See, the millet and the maize are good,' said Noha. 'Though, if this multitude of small birds has its way, little of the grain will ever reach the cooking pots of our people.'

They stooped to pick up the long pole. Tembo's voice was full of concern. 'Behold, the python's tail moves.'

'Have no fear,' laughed Noha. 'It is secured to the pole. Now let me lead. There is a track that greatly shortens our safari. But travel with care – one pace to the left of that path and you are in water up to your waist, half a pace to the right and mud embraces your neck.'

6

Punda and Pili Pili

'Listen!' shouted Tembo. From ahead came the rumble of an earth-moving machine.

'Punda, you and I have in five days done the work of five hundred hoes,' a deep, cheerful voice sang. 'We…' seeing Baruti, Tembo and Noha struggling through the tall elephant grasses with their strange burden, he stopped and leaned out of the window.

They greeted him.

'What is your news?' he replied. Then he saw the python tied to the pole. '*Yoh!*' he laughed. 'That is a way of comfort for a snake to travel.'

Baruti undid the knot in the shirtsleeve that covered the reptile's head. The cold eyes of an indignant python looked at him unwinkingly.

The driver of the machine laughed. 'I am Pili Pili.' He turned to Baruti and the others. 'Punda, who has the strength of a thousand donkeys, joins me in greeting you all. Where do you travel?'

Baruti leaned his end of the pole against the great yellow machine. 'We travel first to the house of the Game Scout and then to see Bwana Kolongo. He…'

'A thing of joy and merit.' Pili Pili slapped his thigh. 'I will save your feet much walking, for at my camp is the jeep which will carry the creature that rests on that pole to Mabwe that he may meet the Area Commissioner Kolongo, who I know has small joy in reptiles. And Punda here, who is an animal of understanding and obedience, will save your feet still further. Let her carry this swallower of goats. Just watch her cleverness.' He pointed to a variety of levers and knobs. 'Pull this: she bends her neck. Push that: she opens her mouth.'

'*Pole pole*, gently, do not let her harm my snake!' shouted Baruti. 'It's filled with shillings – money that means that Tembo here can continue his studies.'

Pili Pili chuckled. 'Is that so? Never fear. Punda has the mouth of a lion but the gentleness of a rabbit.'

He pushed a lever. Baruti guided the pole so that it was grasped in the iron jaws. The snake was swung into the air.

Pili Pili called, 'Come up here with me. The legs of Punda have much strength.'

After they had travelled some distance, Baruti said, 'Since you will deliver this small snake for me we will return to Noha's house in the village of Furahi.'

'It is well,' said Pili Pili. 'Punda and I approve. There is a road that runs into the swamp. Half way it splits. Each part is very much like the other. The swamp on each side is full of the same thick mud and the same tall reeds. But Nungho, the village at one end, is truly called the place of smells and those who live there…' He rolled his eyes expressively. 'But Furahi, the other village, is another matter.'

He swung the wheel and they stopped at a camp, a courtyard surrounded by locked corrugated iron buildings to which was bolted strong steel mesh. Pili Pili unlocked a door and drove a jeep out, parking it close to Punda. He produced a length of rubber hose, one end of which went into the interior of the earth moving machine. The other he covered with a large finger.

'Keep the food for these machines in the large stomach of Punda and the thieves of Nungho are empty handed.' He put the hose and the finger into his mouth and sucked. A large smile suddenly covered his face. 'The inexperienced find their mouths full of the fluid beloved by motors but of small joy to men.' He pushed the hose into the fuel tank of the jeep and removed his finger. Fuel flowed evenly through the hose.

Baruti rolled his eyes. 'How is it that this happens?'

Pili Pili was delighted. 'It is a piece of cunning. Using a tube like this with the end in the tank higher than the other one, then fluid which fills the tube will run uphill before it goes downhill. It is called a siphon.'

'Interesting,' said Baruti. 'Have you more of that tube?'

Pili Pili carefully removed the hose. 'Bwana Kolongo has a great reel with thick hose coiled upon it. Why do you ask?'

'My head fills with ideas,' said Baruti.

A girl came along the road carrying two bowls, one on top of the other. She turned in at the gate.

'Here comes food,' cried Pili Pili. 'Eat with me.'

They had finished their meal when four other Public Works Department men arrived. Pili Pili greeted them. 'You have come at a time of joy. We have a journey to Mabwe and a special visitor for Bwana Kolongo who will be carried with us.'

When they saw the 'visitor' was a snake, his companions lost some of their enthusiasm for the safari. However, when they were sure it was securely tied, they climbed into the jeep. Pili Pili roped the pole to the roof so that the python's head stuck far out beyond the bonnet and its tail was way behind the exhaust pipe. He yelled farewells, and as the headlights cut their way into the night, Baruti, Tembo and Noha trudged on to Furahi.

Noha pointed with his chin. 'Follow that road and you will arrive at Nungho.'

The moon was full. Baruti could see the dark waters on either side of the track. They seemed surrounded with the dank smell of decaying plant life. Frogs and crickets sang a doleful duet. Mosquitoes rose in swarms. Close behind them a hyaena howled and was answered from the Nungho bank. On the night air came the beating of drums in an ugly rhythm that told of death.

Yakobo locked his door as he heard the same drums. There was a tense feeling in the village of Nungho. Hardly a light showed anywhere. As he listened he heard muffled footsteps going past his house. Irritably he switched off his radio and started counting his money to try to forget the disturbing sounds. But, unbidden, his memory recalled the verse, 'What shall it profit a man if he gains the whole world and loses his own soul?'

At last the village merged into an uneasy silence and Yakobo went to bed – but not to sleep. Through his mind the words repeated themselves, 'What shall it profit, what shall it profit…?'

Eighty kilometres away, Pili Pili and his friends were arriving at Mabwe. They swung past the jail.

'Within those walls are Lugu and Dolla,' Pili Pili exclaimed. 'May they long stay out of the Malenga country.' They bumped over the railway line. Soon they were outside the Area Commissioner's house.

An hour before, a weary Nelson Kolongo had gone to bed. He was sound asleep when Pili Pili came to his door calling insistently to be let in. He woke, stumbled out of bed, turned on the light and, yawning widely, opened the front door to be confronted by a group of grinning people holding a large bamboo pole, one

end of which was only an arm's length from his eyes. It was then he saw the python's head. With an effort he stood his ground.

'Bwana A.C.,' grinned Pili Pili, 'Baruti has been at work and he said you would want this one as soon as possible, so we brought him with speed.'

'You did right,' said the Area Commissioner sharply, 'but there is one further thing you must do. Carry this creature to the house of the Americans. It is three gateways to the east. They love reptiles, these people. Take this one there and leave it there.' He closed the door unnecessarily hard.

Pili Pili chuckled. 'Perhaps he has no peace in his stomach. Certainly there is no joy in his head.'

7

Weaver Birds

Dew outlined the huge spider's web. In the dawn light a boy ducked his head under it and scrambled up an anthill that stood a metre above the ripening millet. Grabbing a rope he pulled rhythmically. This rope was attached to strings that stretched out in all directions and to it were tied tins, bells, strips of paper, metal and plastic, pieces of broken bottle – anything that would flutter, glitter or jangle.

Baruti, Noha and Tembo stood watching how this kept the hungry birds in the air.

'It is like a giant spider's web,' breathed Tembo.

Noha nodded and pointed across water and weeds. 'There is the real spider's web, that village of Nungho. It is a kilometre away if you could walk through deep mud and slime, but if you walk on firm ground, five kilometres.'

'That place has been a trap for men for a long time,' said Baruti. 'See the mango trees? They were planted by the Arabs who carried our people away to be slaves over a hundred years ago. These days in the shadow of the same mango trees is the market for marijuana and the fiery drink brewed from honey. These twist people's minds while the cunning ones of Nungho become rich. Many smuggle ivory and rhino horns to buy drugs. Some who enter that evil village disappear forever. It is a place of human spiders.'

Almost with relief, Noha turned sharply to the south. 'High between those trees is the hill beyond the road. The new ways bring small joy to those who live there.'

'We shall go there today,' said Baruti.

He and Tembo had been walking for an hour when they came to a garden with splendid maize growing in soil that had been dug into ridges. Cow manure had been liberally sprinkled over the ground. A young man with a hoe came over to greet them.

'Your corn grows with strength,' smiled Baruti.

'Words of truth. Do I not follow the way of wisdom I learned at school?'

'It is not the custom to use manure,' said Tembo.

The young man laughed. 'It is not the custom of the tribe to have crops like those. Also I do not burn the cornstalks. I dig them in. If only I had water I could have two crops a year.'

Baruti raised his eyebrows. 'Would you have satisfaction if water could be brought to your crops?'

The young gardener rolled his eyes. 'Where would one have luck of that sort?'

Days later and much further round the swamp,

Baruti and Tembo stood looking at a hillside that ran down to the water's edge. The earth was cut and scarred by soil erosion. Above this sick looking piece of ground was a miserable collection of millet.

Baruti greeted a tall thin man. 'What is the news?'

'The news is good, but we face famine. The land hereabouts has no strength.'

'What of the birds?'

The man shrugged. 'We shall have nothing. Neither will they.'

'Your garden would be better if you followed the new way and dug it in ridges so that the rains and the water that runs down from the hill could be held at the roots of your crop. Also, the soil would not be washed away.'

The thin man shrugged. 'It is easier to cut another garden from the thornbush.'

Baruti walked in front, on his shoulder one end of a pole. Tembo carried the other end. On the pole were several bags containing eleven snakes. They walked slowly along the main road.

The earth moving machine came into sight. It stopped and a cheery voice asked, 'What is the news, Bwana Snakecatcher?'

'It's good, Bwana Pili Pili. We have hunted successfully.'

'That is food for the ears. Do you need my help? I often go to Mabwe, and if you tie your snakes in bags with strong rope and firm knots I shall deliver them with care.'

'Thank you very much,' said Baruti. 'This brings me

joy. For these last few days I have heard many words which had no kindness in them.'

'It is understood,' chuckled Pili Pili. 'Those on the far side of the swamp have many goats. Now goats are the enemy of the true farmer. They eat to the roots of the grass and their tongues find seeds deep down. Their hooves cut the ground into many paths and turn solid ground into dust to be carried away by the wind. Woooof! It blows, and the garden is either in the swamp or swirling high in the air on its way to Kenya or even Egypt. Such are the people of the villages of Mutema and Kivunde.'

'Truly,' agreed Baruti. 'These people refuse the idea of using water above and the good earth beneath it.'

'For a time forget these people and bring comfort to your feet and travel with me to the place where Punda rests.'

Rolled in his blanket in Noha's house that evening Tembo whispered, 'Bwana Baruti, I have thankfulness that the great yellow machine took the weight off our feet for many kilometres. Also that our snakes are on the way to those who pay for them.'

Baruti yawned comfortably. 'Sleep with peace, Tembo. Tomorrow we will bring warmth to your heart.'

'Today,' said Noha, still thankful to have been rescued from the python, 'I will show you a way to move through that swamp without wetting your feet.'

At the edge of the water a baobab tree lay on its side. In its gaping hollow trunk was a raft of light wood with four kerosene tins lashed to the underside. White birds stalked around among the reeds in the shade of trees whose upper limbs sagged under the weight of weaver birds' nests.

'Look,' gasped Tembo. 'Look!'

A lithe snake no thicker than a man's thumb was climbing a tree on its way to a dangling nest woven firmly to the end of a branch that was little more than a twig. The entrance to the nest was cunningly placed and shaped so that only with extreme difficulty could any snake take young birds or eggs from it. Seeing their enemy, weaver birds by the score attacked him, some pecking angrily, others fluttering in his face, and all of them shrilling their defiance. The snake couldn't turn. He couldn't strike back so he let go and fell with a splash into the water. They watched him swim away and disappear in the reeds.

'There are many like him,' said Noha, 'Also there are more of those small birds in this swamp than I have ever seen before. Every tree has few leaves but many nests. When the eggs within those nests hatch, millions more weaver birds will fly to the crops. Truly, there will be famine this year.'

Baruti and Tembo saw how true this was as they poled the raft along the strip of water which wound through islands, mud banks, great stones that rose sharply from the water, and the ever-present reeds. The further they went the more birds were there.

'This is a danger that few think about and still fewer know about,' said Baruti. 'Mosquitoes we know, tsetse flies, ordinary flies and ticks that bring us fever.'

'Truly,' agreed Noha. 'There has been trouble with elephants that raid the gardens and baboons that tear the corn from the stalk. But birds in these numbers...' He shrugged expressively and steered the raft onto a sloping patch of mud at the side of an island the size of a football ground. In the straggling trees above them was a colony of noisy little birds with red bills, light brown or yellow feathers and a black collar.

Baruti shook his head. 'I've never seen anything like this before. Are they not thick as locusts when they invade the country? Truly, our people will lose their crop.'

'It is not the people of our country only,' said Noha. 'What hope is there for the harvests of those who live within three days' walk when that army of hungry birds descends upon it?' Noha climbed a large boulder and pointed with his chin. 'There is the Cooking Pot. From close to the water it is hard to see because of the mist that surrounds it.'

Baruti shaded his eyes. 'We must examine that Cooking Pot with care.'

Noha grunted. 'Many would not – especially these days. Strange voices come from it. It is a place of fear. Some who set out to visit it are not seen again.'

Baruti nodded slowly. 'We saw little danger when we flew over it but we moved with the speed of a swallow.'

'Yes,' chimed in Tembo. 'But we did see a large patch of bright green on one side and a black gash near the bottom.'

Baruti interrupted with urgency in his voice. 'Quickly! Let us hide. Men come from the direction of Nungho.'

Hastily they pushed their raft along a narrow channel deep into the reeds and slipped into the water crouching with only their heads showing above the surface.

'I am sinking in the mud,' whispered Tembo.

'You will only go as far as your knees,' breathed Baruti.

'But are there not crocodiles here?'

'Crocodiles are creatures of kindness compared with those from Nungho,' muttered Noha.

'Quiet,' hissed Baruti.

A punt with six men on board went past near enough for them to hear clearly what was being said. Four hundred metres further on, two men leapt off onto a small island and scrambled to the top of a huge boulder which was an ideal lookout post.

Baruti brushed the flies away from his face. 'We must stay as we are till they have returned. Those watchful-eyed ones will see even small movements, but if we are still, all will be well.'

It was difficult to stay still, for they spent hours of torment from flies and mosquitoes and it was not till late afternoon that the punt came out of the mist, picked up the men who were on lookout duty and disappeared in the direction of Nungho.

Baruti, Noha and Tembo returned wearily to Furahi. As they put the raft away Baruti said, 'There is great danger ahead.'

On the far side of the swamp Yakobo closed the shutters in front of his barred windows, shut the door and bolted it. With care he sprayed the room with insecticide, then he sat down and counted his money. The sound of crackling notes helped him to forget the uncomfortable feeling that all was not well. He clung to the thought that his money spelled security to him and opened up the good life.

Yakobo looked round the room and liked what he saw. It was tidy and neat and newly whitewashed. His lip curled as he saw a cockroach move out of a crack in the floor and scuttle up the wall. Yakobo grabbed a knobbed stick and hit the place where the cockroach was with a tremendous crack. Powdery dust exploded into his face, lumps of mud-brick tumbled round his feet and a gaping cavity in the wall yawned at him.

Muttering an Arabic word he had learnt recently, Yakobo sighed and set about cleaning up. 'White ants,' he grunted. 'Beastly brutes.' He swept the debris into a tin and pondered what he would do. 'If Baruti were here,' he mused, 'he'd make some parable out of this. He'd say that a long time ago a couple of ants found their way into those bricks. They increased in number and, working silently, did more and more damage.' He could almost hear Baruti's voice. 'There was one of our helpers who years ago let a small sin slip into his life. He did nothing about it. It became bigger and bigger until...'

Yakobo jumped to his feet angrily. What was he doing letting this sort of thing run through his head? He picked up money from his cupboard, lighted his pressure lamp, locked the door and walked cautiously to the Arab's shop. His mouth was dry and the bucket in his hand shook as he said, 'Hamisi, I want some cement. There are cracks in my floor and cockroaches annoy me.'

'Truly, Bwana Yakobo,' said the shopkeeper, filling the bucket, and then, more softly, 'Why do you not hire a double-barrelled shotgun? Only ten shillings a week. There are many ducks about. Guns bring safety for those with money.'

Yakobo felt much more at ease as he walked back. There was something reassuring about a double-barrelled weapon, for he knew unusual happenings were not uncommon in Nungho. Rumours had reached him of armed robbery, while one day a drunken man, waiting for an injection, had said that in certain cactus patches the witchdoctor's relations regularly threw meat to attract hyaenas. 'Easier than burying people,' the drunken man had hiccupped.

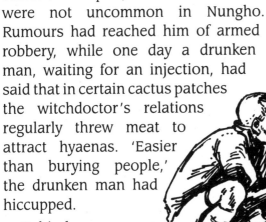

Behind a locked door Yakobo loaded the gun,

then taking it under his arm and a bucket in each hand, he walked in the shadows to a part of the swamp where there was a stretch of sand. He filled the larger bucket with sand and the other with water.

Back in his room he worked hard at repairing the hole in the wall. It was with a sense of great relief that the task was at last finished. How short-lived this would have been had he known that next day both Lugu and Dolla would be released from jail!

8

In The Cooking Pot

Baruti shook Tembo's shoulder and whispered, 'It is the time of second cock-crow. Noha and I are going to the Cooking Pot. The men from Nungho are unlikely to visit it again today. We will return by sunset.'

Tembo wriggled out of his blanket. 'Let me come too.'

Baruti raised his eyebrows. 'Was not yesterday enough?'

The boy shook his head.

It was well before dawn when they moved through thick mist to the raft. With the coming of the sun the mist lifted. Ahead loomed the side of the Cooking Pot. A wide channel separated it from the reed-covered mud of the side of the swamp.

'For three kilometres,' said Noha, 'these reeds grow as thick as the hairs on a lion's neck, right up to where the railway is built. In them are millions of nests and more weaver birds than any man could count.'

Baruti turned to the crater. 'This Pot must be nearly a kilometre long and all its sides are high as a giraffe.'

They paddled the raft along the channel between rock and reeds and rounded the far end. There was only one place to land. They dragged the raft up to the rim where they stood dumb with amazement. Every tree within sight was weighed down with weaver birds' nests. Every twig had its own nest. They stared at the inside of the Pot sloping down sharply from them.

'This is like a giant ant hill turned upside down.' Tembo had to shout to be heard above the clamour of the birds.

Baruti's voice boomed out, 'Into the stomach of these jabberers will go the food that should fill a thousand thousand cooking pots. Bwana Kolongo must hear about this quickly. There are dozens of nests on the islands of the swamp but here are hundreds – thousands of them.'

They forced their way round the rim of the crater. A mirage-like haze made this strange, red-brown, rock-lined hole merge into the pattern of the swamp.

Baruti pushed through tall, dry grass and stood on a cleared spot. He whistled with surprise as he saw a tin with a rope attached above a drain, which led to a vivid green patch. Noha scrambled down and looked at the plants. 'It is the hemp plant from which comes marijuana. The men we saw yesterday were watering the stuff,' Noha shouted.

Baruti nodded. 'It's easy to understand why those of Nungho wish to frighten the people who live around the edge of the swamp. They are experts at telling stories of terror – of evil spirits, of fierce creatures that roar and of men who disappear.' He picked up a coil of rope. 'Come, let us visit these ghosts and the dark gash in the ground which we saw from above.'

They hacked a path towards the bottom of the crater through thick grass and thornbush scrub. They chopped off scores of limbs weighed down by nests which dangled almost to the ground. The noise of the birds was unbearably shrill.

Near the bottom of the crater the trees thinned out but the dry grass was waist-high to the very edge of a long black hole. Noha picked up a stone and threw it. There was the odd, echoing sound of a stone being dropped into a clay pot. Moving cautiously to the edge they peered down.

'It has a bottom that isn't far below,' said Baruti. He tied one end of his rope cunningly to a root where it could not be seen from above and threw the coil down. They heard it land. Baruti squeezed his way between two rocks, gripped the rope and said, 'I'm going down.'

He was only two metres over the edge when a loud, hissing rumble came from below. Dust, small stones and grass eddied round him. He hung on desperately and shouted, 'This is no ghost, not even a huge snake. It is merely the wind blowing through a long tunnel.' Again he lowered himself, cautiously, dangling for a long, anxious moment and grunting with relief when his feet touched solid ground. He was in a large bottle-shaped cave. His legs straddled a long, dark crack through the rock floor.

Noha's anxious voice reached him from above. 'Baruti, those of Nungho are at the top. They have found our raft and are tearing it to pieces. Soon they will come searching for us.'

Baruti's voice came eerily from below. 'Climb down even as I have done. They will not find us here.'

Noha and Tembo were quickly beside him. They crouched together, well out of sight. Then came shouting from above.

A voice announced, 'They have jumped into the crack in the Pot. It is well known that no one goes down there and ever comes back.'

Baruti chuckled softly and Noha whispered, 'Listen.' There was a hissing noise gradually growing louder. With a shriek, a blast of air swept through the crack in the floor. Dust swirled around in the cave. Before they could draw a breath it happened all over again but more forcefully still.

'Let's go,' shouted a voice. 'This is a place of hostile spirits.' There was the sound of stumbling feet and then the ear-splitting chattering of the sparrow-sized birds.

'It would be a thing of wisdom to stay here quietly,' whispered Baruti. 'Probably there are those that watch.'

An hour went by, then voices came again. Broken pieces of their raft were hurled down from above and, as if in reply, a strong gust of wind came howling through the crack in the floor. So loud was it that the wood and tins hardly made a sound as they landed. Again there was confused shouting and the noise of thousands of indignant weaver birds.

After a long pause Tembo said, 'Now we have no raft.'

Noha nodded. 'But we can crawl up to the other side of the Cooking Pot and drop into the water after it is dark. It is but a small swim to the other side.'

There was fear in Tembo's voice, 'There we will find a long stretch of mud which will suck us down with certainty.'

Noha shook his head. 'I saw a place where there was a large, flat rock. Perhaps the mist hid it from you, but I can find it even in the dark.

'Behold, we have much time to wait before we prove what you say,' said Baruti, picking up some of the porous wood and pushing it into the long crack.

'What we need is water,' said Noha, 'then it would swell and block up the whole gap. That would silence the ghosts.'

Baruti yawned. 'We have got enough wood to block half of it. Let us rest. There are still two hours to midday.'

For long hours they crouched uncomfortably in the cave, not speaking above a whisper for fear that one of the Nungho cut-throats was waiting and watching above. At last darkness came and Baruti climbed the rope, making sure that all was safe before hauling up the others.

The swim across from the Cooking Pot to the rock was a nightmare. At last they struggled through slimy mud and reeds to the security of a long flat rock.

'Truly,' muttered Baruti, 'I prayed.'

'And I,' nodded Noha.

Tembo was too exhausted to speak. The men gathered some reeds and spread them out. 'We will lie on some of these and cover ourselves with others,' said Noha. 'They will make the rock seem softer.'

'Truly,' grunted Baruti, 'it will be better to give a meal to a million mosquitoes than to one crocodile.'

Tembo forced a smile. 'It was that one crocodile I was thinking about during that terrible swim through those dark waters.'

9

Complications

Yonah, the game scout, came to the door of his house. Three bedraggled figures came towards him. 'You look as though you have spent a night of small comfort.'

Baruti whistled quietly. 'You speak words that make me feel I am again trying to sleep on a hard rock in the middle of that swamp in cold darkness.'

Yonah chuckled. 'While we wait for food, tell me what brings you here at this hour looking as you do.'

Baruti sighed. 'It started this time yesterday. We went very early to the Cooking Pot of Ghosts which goes down deep into the ground. It is rock. The rim is the height of three men and there is only one place to climb it from the water. We were interested to find there a garden of Indian hemp.'

Yonah nodded. 'It is the work of Nungho.'

'Exactly,' agreed Baruti. 'But we walked with feet full of caution to a hole near the lower part of the Pot. It looks like the open mouth of a snake.'

'Some say it is bottomless,' broke in Yonah.

'We took no chances,' laughed Baruti, 'for we threw in pebbles to see how deep it was. They rattled like beans in a gourd. Then it was we heard voices full of anger. Those of Nungho had come seeking us, but we hid in this cave of darkness. Above us we heard loud voices, but these were drowned by a deep booming sound that came from the long crack in the stone floor.

Yonah chuckled. 'Truly, that Pot has stomach that gives it no joy.'

Baruti nodded. 'Noha, Tembo and I felt fear creeping under our skin but those who sought us had the kind of fear that sent them to the top of the Pot with speed. But for safety we waited until darkness.'

'And what then?' asked Yonah.

Noha shuddered as he remembered. 'We crawled through thorns and over sharp pebbles. We jumped into dark waters and swam with the fear of the nearness of crocodiles. We waded in the darkness through mud and slime and spent the night on a cold rock.'

'Ugh,' shuddered Yonah. 'Mocked by frogs and crickets while you provided a feast for mosquitoes. That has happened before to others. But come, we must listen to the orders of that man of action, Kolongo.' He switched on the radio. An authoritative voice spoke in Swahili.

'Calling Game Scout Yonah Nhuti. It is the second hour – 8 a.m. Are you receiving me? Over.'

'Receiving you loud and clear, Bwana Kolongo. Over.'

'I am arriving at 10 a.m. Expecting report from Baruti. We are looking for action. Over and out.'

The jail clock showed 8 a.m. The door opened and out stepped two men. One looked disgruntled, the other was plump and smiling. He rubbed his hands together and slapped his companion on the shoulder.

'Bwana Dolla, what we need is money – lots of it.'

'But how?' rasped Dolla.

'Leave this to Winston Churchill Lugu,' chuckled the plump man, adjusting his neat green hat. 'Money grows for those who know where to look for it.'

He shaded his eyes against the morning sun. A lorry was lumbering towards them. He raised his hat, pointed his thumb in the direction that the lorry was travelling and smiled. The vehicle shot past them. They were engulfed in red suffocating dust.

'*Kah*!' snarled Dolla. 'He takes no notice. He…'

'Peace,' retorted his companion. 'Look, even now he pulls up. Leave the talking to me.' He walked towards the lorry and greeted the Arab driver courteously in Swahili. 'Good day to you. My name is Winston Churchill Lugu. I'm a business man. Could you give us a lift towards Nungho?'

'Have you two shillings each?' queried the driver.

'*Ahah*,' laughed Lugu. 'I have better than that.'

On the far side of the lorry Dolla swung himself up and had the door open in a trice. The lorry driver grabbed a tyre lever and waved it threateningly.'

'Nobody cheats Hamid bin Aziz. I want my money now or out you get!'

'Peace,' said Lugu. 'Hamid, what are four miserable shillings? We can show you how to make hundreds and hundreds of them.'

The driver looked at him quickly. Lugu's laughter came reassuringly. 'It sounds good, doesn't it? Lots of lovely money. Think of it. Think of what you can do with it. We have some special things to sell to those who have a desire for them.'

The driver put down the tyre lever. 'Well, get in.'

Lugu did so briskly. The Arab started the engine and growled, 'Where is all this money that you talk about?'

The plump man raised his eyebrows. 'My wealth is here.' He tapped his head. 'You have a need. We have the answer.'

The driver spat and they hurtled forward. There was a long silence. Dolla started to speak but Lugu's elbow hit him hard in the ribs.

They were going down a steep hill above the swamp country. Ahead was a hairpin bend in the road. The Arab clamped on his brakes. Nothing happened. Blocking half of the road was a large notice: HATARI. DANGER. The lorry crashed into it, skidded, swung across into the jungle, toppled sideways and stopped with a jerk, propped up by a large cactus. Hamid's door burst open. He shot out, cracking his head heavily on it. In a second Lugu was bending over him. He pulled off the Arab's coat, folded it and placed it under his head and fanned him with his hat. After some minutes the Arab's eyes flickered and he sat up looking bewildered.

'You see what I mean,' chuckled Lugu. 'We bring you good luck. I have a charm that never fails. Agreed, a bang on the head is never welcome but there is no real damage done to you or the machine. My companion, Dolla, has hit his head against the roof. This will not improve his outlook on life. But, never mind, I see you have a strong winch. Let us use it and get back onto the road.'

They spent the next half hour easing the lorry back onto the road. Lugu carefully wiped his hands on a snow-white handkerchief which had once been the property of the governor of the jail. Dolla came across and muttered to him.

Lugu nodded and they climbed back into the lorry and moved at much slower speed. When they arrived, he said, 'Oh Hamid, my friend and I have saved you very considerable expense. We ask no payment and will give you none.'

They drove along in hostile silence. Coming to a side road Lugu ordered, 'Stop!'

The Arab muttered and put on his brakes. Lugu and Dolla jumped down and walked off without a word.

The driver rubbed his head, shouted unmentionable things in Arabic and drove off.

'*Koh*,' mumbled Dolla, 'here we are with no money and nowhere to go. Nothing. A lot of use that is to an empty stomach and an empty pocket.'

'Peace,' smiled Lugu, 'Take heart.'

They stepped off the road as another lorry rattled past towards Nungho. Dolla cursed the dust but Lugu looked with interest at the vehicle.

'Ram Singh, Builder and Contractor,' he read. 'What would he be doing at a place like Nungho?'

Dolla made no reply to his queries but he had much to say regarding headaches, heat and flies.

They came to a large fig tree. Lugu sat down on one of the roots. 'Let us rest for a while,' he said. And, as Dolla threw himself down muttering, Lugu continued, 'Things are not as bad as you had thought. When our friend lay unconscious I found some small profit in his pocket. Your mouth was full of words of misery but Lugu as usual was on the job.'

He produced five ten shilling notes. Dolla snatched at them but he was far too slow. Lugu smiled. 'I left another five where he fell. Before long when the fog goes from his brain he will return and there will be his money. He will blame the wind for what he cannot find, not us.'

'*Kah*!' Dolla spat viciously. 'A waster of money you are.'

'Play safely,' purred Lugu. 'Always play safely.' He proceeded to do so. 'Beyond those mango trees is a house where there is food and friendship.'

They went to a house built on the edge of the swamp.

'*Lete pombe*, bring beer!' shouted Dolla.

At once he started to drink to celebrate his release from jail, while Lugu asked a string of questions which concerned Yakobo's activities, marijuana, ivory and rhino horns.

By midday Dolla was asleep but Lugu was carefully observing Yakobo's house. He watched with interest as person after person came for injections.

10
Yakobo Sinks Deeper

Precisely on time the Area Commissioner's Land Rover arrived. He stepped down and greeted those waiting for him, then turned to two men who were with him. 'Sergeant, warm up the radio phone.' To the man in the mechanic's overalls, 'Meshak, get that machine going.'

Pili Pili stepped forward. 'Bwana, Punda is sick. She has worked with the strength of ten elephants. She...'

The corners of Kolongo's mouth twitched. 'See that she is repaired. Now, Game Scout, your report please.'

Yonah saluted smartly. 'These men of experience have words of special importance.'

'I will hear them first. Tell me the whole matter.'

The army sergeant walked over and stood in the background. For fifteen minutes the A.C. listened carefully, nodding from time to time and firing sharp questions.

He spoke thoughtfully, 'Let me summarise. For six weeks you have travelled the Malenga country from end to end and from side to side.'

'We have also caught thirty-seven interesting snakes,' burst out Tembo.

Nelson Kolongo smiled. 'Forget the snakes. The harvest matters most. First we must deal with the problem of the feathered thieves of what is ripening now. Then we have some data on what we need to do in preparing for the future – draining, water storage, irrigation, road building. Then there are the complications: the less progressive farmers of the area, the criminals, the growers, users and sellers of marijuana, the poachers and ivory dealers.'

Baruti nodded. 'Our visit to the Cooking Pot and our escape from it makes me feel that there is a simple way of storing water and using it with profit.'

The A.C. was indulgent. 'You do not know the ways of government, but maybe you're right.'

Noha spoke quietly, 'I have a word to say, Bwana. A road could easily be made to the Cooking Pot for there are many islands of rock close together. They are wide enough for two trucks to pass each other and half way is one particular place shaped like the half moon with much stone upon it.'

'Where does this path start and finish?' demanded Kolongo.

'It begins within twenty paces of the Pot itself and comes out in the reeds close to the house of Yonah Nhuti. You enter it near a great stone shaped like an egg.'

Kolongo glanced at his watch. 'I must call the Veterinary and Agricultural Officers and the Engineer.'

Over the air a minute later went brisk messages. 'Meet me outside the Game Scout's office near Saba Railway Station at 11.30 hours. Over and out.' The A.C. put down the microphone and looked across at the Game Scout. 'Now, your report, please.'

Yonah saluted. 'There is ivory hidden in or near Nungho. The bones of three dead elephants have been found. No news of where the ivory is hidden.'

'But do you think it is at Nungho?' asked the A.C.

Yonah grunted. 'Where else, Bwana? But how to find it is another thing.'

'You need additional help. More about that later. Now, for a quick safari to the Cooking Pot.'

The sergeant saluted. 'We need a raft to take us there. We have six suitable oil drums, but we need timber.'

Pili Pili came across from the shed. 'Bwana Kolongo,' he called. 'It is a thing of joy. Punda's sickness is cured. That expert is a man of wisdom!'

'Enough!' broke in Kolongo. 'The sergeant needs timber.'

Pili Pili nodded his head vigorously. 'There was a time when the house of Punda had doors made from wood. Excellent doors, and strong, but not strong enough for the axes of the thieving ones from Nungho who would steal the food from Punda's stomach. The doors were replaced by strong steel that takes the teeth from a file.'

'Yes, yes. But what about the timber?'

'I was coming to that, Bwana A.C. The wood rests in Punda's house. It would sit with comfort on oil drums. Also there is a large roll of wire which I happened to find one day.'

Kolongo looked at the speaker with a guarded twinkle in his eyes. 'Proceed with the work, Sergeant.'

Noha stepped forward. 'There is a breeze that comes after the heat of midday that will fill our sails and blow us with strength towards the Cooking Pot.'

A loud backfire came from the shed. Kolongo jumped. 'Punda awakes,' laughed Baruti, poking his head round the door. 'She will pull a trailer with the oil drums and the doors.'

The large yellow machine, spick and span and shining like new, rumbled into the sunlight.

'An excellent man that,' said Kolongo quietly to the sergeant. 'It's amazing the work he can coax out of that machine. We can do a useful project at small cost.'

The drums were rapidly loaded and the doors wedged between them. Baruti noticed with satisfaction that three lengths of hose were tucked into a corner of the trailer.

The A.C. glanced at his wrist watch. 'At 11.00 hours exactly I must make a number of contacts on the radio phone. We have five minutes to wait. After that, Game Scout, we will visit Nungho.'

Yakobo looked unhappily round his room. His clock pointed to five minutes to eleven. On the floor lay Dolla snoring. He had thumped at the door sometime near first cock crow and had stumbled in, very drunk. At dawn he had been miserably sick.

The routine existence that Yakobo valued greatly was gone. Lugu was sitting busily turning the knobs of the transistor radio. People were coming up the path for injections. It was impossible to work with the place in this mess.

Yakobo felt his temper building up. He shouted, 'Lugu, put down that radio. Take Dolla and clear out!'

Lugu merely smiled. His hand went into his pocket. 'I agree with you. Dolla is a pest, but he has his uses. Remember that I am not a sleeping partner.' He glanced down at the snoring man. 'This radio is our ears. It can save us from trouble.' Abruptly his suave tone became a snarl. There was a knife in his hand. 'And don't you raise your voice to me!'

He paused as the radio crackled and announced, 'This is Area Commissioner calling Veterinary Officer. Calling District Agricultural Officer. Calling Public Works Department Engineer. I am visiting the Malenga district investigating weaver bird situation and implementing plans for swamp control. Will you all be available at 16.30 hours for consultation at the Game Scout's post near Saba Railway Station? I shall repeat that.

'Also, I have information that there is ivory hidden in the Nungho area. We will be visiting the portion of the swamp known as Cooking Pot of Ghosts and I plan an immediate surprise visit to Nungho. Over and out.'

A new voice came on the air. 'Mabwe Police calling A.C. Are you reading me? Over.'

'Area Commissioner reading you loud and clear. Over.'

'Heard your message re: ivory. Patrols on Great North Road have been notified. Over and out.'

Lugu left the radio switched on. 'Now perhaps you will understand this radio device is not for your entertainment at the moment. It is our ears. It's our completely safe, completely unexpected way of knowing what Kolongo is doing.' He sneered at the people squatting under a tree waiting for injections. 'Get on with it. Give those fools their injections of... Why don't you make it milk and water and save your penicillin for those who will really pay for it? Inject them. Don't waste time. I'll collect the money. We mustn't be visible when that busybody arrives but we must have money. Follow my way and you'll be rich.'

Yakobo said nothing but gave the injections. Lugu pocketed the money. His face was suddenly all smiles. 'Now be a good fellow and make yourself scarce till after sundown. You're in a slippery spot. Do you think Kolongo will let you get away with borrowing that penicillin? Why, he'd be delighted to turn you into an example to healthy-minded young men in the medical services he's so proud of. Don't you see? You're just the one to be a stern warning to those who think to increase their thin wages by a little hard-to-notice theft.'

Yakobo remained silent while carefully packing the penicillin equipment into a suitcase. He looked up as a click sounded behind him. Lugu had sidled across the room, grabbed the shotgun and loaded it. Still smiling he said, 'I shall look after this with special care.' He thumped the butt on the floor close to Dolla's head.

He blinked, grunted and sat up.

Lugu's voice cracked like a whip. 'Kolongo will be here any minute and you snore your way back to jail.' He watched Yakobo pick up an obviously new red fez, place it carefully on his head and walk out of the door.

'Come, Dolla,' Lugu rasped. 'Let's get out of here. You and I have work to do in the matter of elephant's tusks. The safest place for us is where we can watch the movements of this well-educated and public-spirited young government official.' He carefully locked the door and put a padlock on the bolt.

Yakobo crossed the track and forced his way through undergrowth until he came to a slope above the place where the road to Nungho and Furahi joined the main road. He pushed past a thornbush. A branch swung back and hit him across the cheek. Startled with pain, he stooped to pick up his red hat and a carefully wrapped brown paper parcel that was in it.

Wiping the blood from his face he walked on. Thorns always made him think of Jesus Christ. The crown of thorns they had forced down on Jesus' forehead must have been intensely painful, but nothing to be compared with the spikes they had used to nail him to the cross…

Deliberately Yakobo stopped this chain of thought. He took the brown paper parcel, untied the string and counted three thousand shillings. He chuckled. It sounded as though Lugu had expected to find money in the penicillin box but he, Yakobo, had been one step ahead.

He stopped under a large baobab tree, retied the parcel and swung himself high into the branches. With a smile of satisfaction he came on a hollow where a limb had broken off. There was the sound of crumbling wood. His fingers still gripped the parcel of money. Carefully he started to pull it back towards him. When it was almost out, his fingers slipped and he heard the faint sound of the parcel landing inside the hollow of the ancient tree.

Muttering angrily, Yakobo climbed down and walked around the base. Often there was a hole at ground level. The stench of dead flesh struck his nose. Between the trunk and an ant's nest a looped wire snare had been placed. An unfortunate hyaena had pushed his head through. The way the wretched creature lay showed how it had jerked back with all its strength and tugged and struggled in a frenzy of pain.

Yakobo's imagination filled in a vivid picture and, promptly, words that covered it came into his mind. 'Thorns and snares are in the path of the rebellious. He that keeps his soul shall be far from them.' What a fool he had been to learn the book of Proverbs by heart! He spat and, covering his nose with his hand, stepped over the dead creature. There was no opening in the tree. He'd have to hack a hole through the trunk – but not now. The sound of an axe would only attract the inquisitive. He comforted himself that there could be no better hiding place for his money than inside that huge, thousand-year-old tree.

Down the road came the A.C.'s jeep, followed by Pili Pili's large yellow machine and a Land Rover towing a heavily loaded trailer. Baruti and Tembo sat beside Pili Pili on the earth moving machine.

Pili Pili chuckled. 'A most unusual creature is my Punda. I could sing you a song of her achievements. Also, if I were singing there would be a verse about Bwana Kolongo who never uses six words when three will do – one who sees more with his one eye than most people do with two. Within his head is the wisdom and the cunning and the skill of Punda himself. He will go to Nungho and stop at the shop of Hamisi. He will ask a few questions and say a few words about ivory and rhino horns and, because of them, Nungho will boil like a pot full of porridge and there will be uncertainty in the minds of those who spit on the law.'

As if to prove him right Kolongo went into Hamisi's shop watched by scores of eyes, including those of Lugu and Dolla.

The A.C. said with deliberation, 'Did you hear that the police are on the lookout for ivory poachers? We're searching for those who give illegal injections. If anyone is housing them they will be in trouble. The same applies to anyone involved with rhino horns or ivory.'

The Arab trader bowed. 'I shall indeed report any criminal activity to you, Mr Area Commissioner.'

Nelson Kolongo gave him a long, hard look and drove off in the direction of Furahi.

11

Thugs

The door of Yakobo's room was wide open. A note lay on the floor. Lugu picked it up and read, 'Gone to Mabwe to collect two hundred shillings.' Lugu tore it up and threw it on the floor. He glanced round the room. Nothing seemed to have been touched. He made a careful search but there was no sign of money. He sniffed the box where the penicillin had been and there was the unmistakable smell of bank notes.

Lugu sat down and said aloud. 'You're slipping, Winston Churchill Lugu. You've let that Dolla take Yakobo's wealth from under your nose. Greedy fool! He is after the other hoard at the hospital. He'll pay for this.'

Step by step he worked out Dolla's movements. Then a tight little smile spread round his lips. He picked up his walking stick and strolled down to the swamp.

Dolla pedalled hard down the path that led to the main road. Yakobo sat despondently gazing ahead of him. Down the road rumbled the ancient bus that would reach Mabwe in about two hours. Towards it came a man riding a bicycle furiously. Yakobo sprang up as he recognised both machine and rider. Dolla had taken his bicycle!

Dolla swung the wheel towards the swamp and raced to jump on the crowded vehicle. The bicycle slowly slid towards the water. Yakobo dashed down the hill shouting. Thorns tore at him. He tripped over a vine and fell heavily. With a splash the machine fell into the deep channel beside the road.

Yakobo kicked off his shoes and dived again and again, deep into the muddy water. Groping along the bottom he at last found the bicycle but it had sunk so far into the slime he couldn't drag it out. Wet and furious, he hurried the three dusty kilometres to Nungho but his room was shut and locked. It took time to borrow rope. The walk back to the main road blistered his feet.

Yakobo tied the rope to a tree and dived in the exact spot where he knew the bicycle was. But in the time he had been away it had sunk deeper and, though he tried desperately, his efforts were useless. Angry and dispirited and dripping wet, he limped back to find his door still locked. As the sun set, mosquitoes in hordes descended upon him.

Dolla's safari was a series of successes. He arrived within sight of the hospital by sunset and strode through the gates and into the ward. It was the time of the evening meal. Everyone was busy. No one took any notice of him. He dropped his hat in the middle of the ward, bent down and fumbled under the table.

There was the package stuck firmly in place. He pulled it away, put it into his pocket, stood up and walked out of the door.

Dolla walked back and sat by the road in the shadows. 'If you have enough nerve you can get away with anything,' he thought. 'No one has any idea where I am or what I've been doing.' It pleased him to feel that he was a step ahead of Lugu and streets in front of Kolongo.

Dr Matama looked through the window of the hospital office. Against the red sky he saw a familiar figure walk through the gate.

Over the radio phone Nelson Kolongo's voice was giving a concise account of the weaver bird battle. 'And that's how the situation stands at the moment. Over,' he said.

The doctor picked up the microphone.

'Daudi Matama speaking. I have just seen Dolla walking furtively into the hospital. He is forbidden to visit without permission. I know he troubles you even more than he does us. Over.'

Four hours later Dolla had spent a thousand shillings on a green plastic suitcase packed with marijuana, avoided two police road blocks and found an old friend who for a suitable sum of money had driven him back to Nungho.

Lugu strolled back to Yakobo's room. The sun was poised above the horizon. On the doorstep sat a bedraggled Yakobo. There were jagged tears in his shirt and shorts. His fine gold watch with the date window looked very out of place on his mud-stained wrist.

Lugu came up softly. 'You're in trouble, Bwana Yakobo. You've been through deep water.' He chuckled at his joke, unlocked the door, lit the primus stove, put on the kettle, lighted the lamp, cut bread, buttered it and smeared it with honey.

Yakobo stumbled in through the door and slumped down in a chair without saying a word. The kettle started to sing. 'My kettle,' he thought. Lugu dexterously heated the pot, put half a handful of tea into it and poured on boiling water. Yakobo, through half-closed eyes, saw what was happening and muttered, 'My teapot and my tea.' And, as Lugu poured it, 'My cups and my condensed milk and my sugar.'

'Have a cup of tea and some food,' invited Lugu. 'It will do you good.'

Yakobo grunted and took it. The hot fluid was comforting and the bread and honey certainly showed him his hunger.

Lugu's voice was full of solicitude. 'Now sleep would be the wise thing. Tomorrow could be a difficult day. Look at the time. Let us keep up with the activities of the government.'

'With my transistor radio,' growled Yakobo as he stood up, put half a kerosene tin full of water on the primus and threw himself heavily back into the chair. He took little interest in Kolongo's various radio conversations.

Suddenly he heard a voice he had wanted to hear for weeks coming through the radio set. 'Daudi Matama speaking. Dolla has completely disappeared from here. Rumour is that he had thousands of shillings with him. Over and out.'

'Dolla,' growled out Yakobo. 'I'll give him Dolla. He threw my bicycle into the swamp.'

Lugu was listening with a smile playing round the corners of his mouth. 'Bwana Yakobo, it has been a hard day. We all have our reverses. For this reason I have taken lodging tomorrow for us both at the house of Nyale, who spends much of his time making a drink of peculiar strength from honey. Drink sufficient and life appears golden.'

'I know it,' said Yakobo harshly. 'Drink another gourd full and you're dead.'

Lugu shrugged, wrapped himself in his blanket and lay down. But before he went to sleep his mind ruminated. 'All this noise about bicycles and not a word about money. Yakobo has tried to be smart. Almost certainly the money is hidden somewhere close. I must get him out of the way and have a thorough search.' He yawned and almost at once was asleep.

But Yakobo could not sleep. From Nungho came the sound of drums. Foreboding hovered over him. A loose sheet of iron on the roof rattled. Wind surged through the mango trees. A frog croaked on and on in slow, sad rhythm like the drum that was beaten when a chief had died.

How long ago was it since he had been really happy? Three days ago he had had money, more than he knew what to do with. People had treated him with respect. He had a feeling of power. Then the situation had changed as quickly and definitely as his bicycle had disappeared into the mud of the swamp. But was everything to be lost as finally as that bicycle? There was still time to collect many of the things which had seemed to bring him contentment. He still had enough penicillin and equipment to start over again in some other place. It would definitely be safer to earn more money and buy again the things which had been stolen. He closed his eyes. Sleep seemed closer.

He started up shocked by the harsh, tearing sound of the wind dragging at the sheet of loose corrugated iron. Shadows moved on the wall opposite him. Vividly he lived again the moment when that wall, looking so solid and secure, had crumbled and gaped open under a blow aimed to kill an insect. In the distance a hyaena howled. Its voice moved further and further away and Yakobo drifted back into troubled sleep. Again he was hiding his roll of notes in the trunk of the baobab tree. Again there for all to see was the loop of the snare in the path. Hyaena saw the snare, smelt something that attracted him greatly and walked open-eyed into the deadly wire. His nightmare became a frenzied tangle of horror. From just outside came a hyaena's ugly laugh, high-pitched and hysterical.

Yakobo sat up in a sweat. 'I'm the one who's trapped,' he muttered. Everything that he had thought solid or secure or satisfying was falling apart. He shuddered as he thought of the dead hyaena. Was death offering him a way out of this hopelessness? Why had God let this happen to him?

For a moment his mind turned to Jesus Christ. Familiar words hammered in his brain. 'Don't save riches on earth where moths and rust spoil and thieves break in and steal. Instead, save riches in heaven where moths and rust cannot spoil nor thief steal, for where your riches are you may be certain that your heart will be too. No one can be loyal to two chiefs.'

For the first time he realised that contentment had begun to drain from his life when he had started to follow out only such of God's instructions as suited him. He would like to experience that feeling of contentment once again.

There was a movement in the other side of the room. Lugu had switched on the torch and was pulling on his shoes. He put on his coat.

Yakobo almost shouted, 'What are you doing?'

'Ah, good morning,' said Lugu. 'It is the early bird who catches the worms. I am out to make profit. Come with me and we'll make lots of beautiful money.'

Yakobo stood up and spat.

'Peace,' said Lugu. 'What do you plan to do?'

The question swept into Yakobo's mind, 'What can I do? I'm finished.' Again came the picture of the hyaena and the snare.

Lugu's voice broke in. 'Come along with me. I can hide you at Nyale's house and we'll do our work after dark.'

'They loved darkness rather than light because their deeds were evil' flashed instantly into Yakobo's mind. He felt the wire of his own snare tightening around him.

'You're closing doors for yourself,' said Lugu. 'Go back to your old haunts and it's jail for you. Go back to your precious hospital and it's the sack. Walk any street in any town in Tanzania and before a week is out a policeman will put his hand on your shoulder.'

The desire to hit the owner of that suave voice was almost overwhelming. Yakobo picked up the kerosene bottle. Just in time he saw the glint of Lugu's knife ready in his hand. Again came that odious throaty chuckle. 'It would seem that you have chosen your own path. Goodbye.' He sprang through the door. Yakobo threw himself forward but the bolt was shot and the padlock clicked.

Yakobo sat down and tried to think calmly. If he wrenched the leg off the table he could bend the bar of the window and force his way out. He turned up the wick of the lamp. Slowly he packed his clothes, the kettle and the alarm clock. He thought of the things which had already gone. He folded his blanket and placed it in the suitcase on top of penicillin and syringes.

'Things could be worse,' he told himself. 'Lugu's words are frightening but they are not the whole truth. I won't make the same mistake again, and there are many other towns in East Africa.'

Lugu walked smartly down the hill towards Nyale's house. In the gloom he saw two shadowy figures moving towards him.

'Good morning,' he said. Both men stopped when they saw the blade of his knife. 'An ideal time of the day for a small amount of well-paid work that I would like you to do for me. Fifty shillings each and all I ask is that you break in the door of the house of the one who till recently gave injections of penicillin. To earn your money, beat him up thoroughly. What you do when you have finished is not my concern. You understand?'

Their answer was two grunts, then, 'How shall we get in?' growled a voice.

'With a reasonably large stone you could crack that door off its hinges.' In the darkness Lugu's walking stick could easily have been confused with a firearm. 'I shall stand at a suitable spot and make sure you do the job properly.'

One of the men spat and the other said, 'Give us the money.'

'Half of it is yours now,' said Lugu, 'the other half when I see you carrying him past me.'

The two figures melted into the darkness.

There was a tremendous thump on Yakobo's door. He looked round for a weapon, grabbed a chair and swung it above his head. With a noise like a gun shot the door burst in. Two burly figures dashed through the dust and splinters. Yakobo swung his chair at the foremost, who flung a handful of sand into his eyes. Yakobo dropped the chair. The second thug hit him hard on the knee cap with a knobbed stick. The agony of this blow made him stumble forward. The first man deliberately picked up the chair and brought it down with great force on his victim's head. Yakobo heard the chair crack into pieces and then darkness surged over him.

Without a word one took his arms and the other his legs and they moved as fast as they could towards the swamp.

Lugu seemed to materialise from the darkness. 'Is he dead?'

The first man nodded. 'He's already greeting his ancestors. You should have heard his head crack. It sounded like dropping an egg.'

Lugu held out more money, lifted Yakobo's limp arm and took off his wrist watch and asked, 'What are you going to do with him now?'

'The safest way to bury him is to throw him into the swamp. There is no more suitable grave than the stomach of the crocodile,' sneered the taller of the two thugs.

They walked four hundred paces to the edge of the water then, swinging Yakobo's body back, they hurled it as far as they were able into the swamp.

The coldness of the water shocked Yakobo back into consciousness. There was fiery pain in the back of his head and one of his knees would not move. Automatically he floated on his back. The before-dawn breeze blew eerily through the reeds. He heard a voice say, 'Well, that's the end of him. Penicillin does little for cracked skulls.'

Still lying on his back and barely moving his hands he swam backstroke. His head bumped agonizingly against a tuft of reeds. The beam of a torch moved this way and that across the stagnant water. He took a deep breath and drew himself under the surface. He stayed under as long as he could. When he surfaced, to his great relief, the light had gone. The pain in his knee was severe and cramps were dragging at the calves of his legs. He pulled himself through the mud, struggled up the bank, limped somehow across the road, then forced his way through the undergrowth to a pile of granite boulders that hid him from the road. Behind these he again collapsed into unconsciousness.

12
Man or Bird?

The Area Commissioner pulled up in the middle of Furahi village. He greeted the crowd which had gathered and walked to where the raft was taking shape.

Kolongo called Pili Pili. 'There is a safari ahead of that donkey of yours. Go round the swamp to the place mentioned this morning and look the place over.'

'Punda agrees,' said Pili Pili. 'Also I shall attempt to distil her wisdom. And talking of distilling,' he dropped his voice so that only the A.C. could hear, 'did you smell that smell at Nungho? Somebody turns honey into that drink of fire which sends man's wisdom on safari.' Kolongo raised his eyebrows.

Baruti came from the carpenter's house staggering under an armful of very long bamboo poles. Nelson Kolongo walked over towards him. 'Baruti, we only need two or three of those.'

The hunter put down his load. 'Great One, in my

mind has grown a thought. I watched Pili Pili fill the tank of the jeep from the still larger tank of that large yellow creature of his. He told me how water could be made to flow uphill and then downhill if there was more downhill than up.'

'True,' smiled the A.C., 'we call this syphoning.'

'These bamboo poles,' said Baruti, 'can be made hollow like pipes. We might well turn this Cooking Pot from a place where famine is born to a huge pot filled with water which could irrigate most excellent land. The crops of rice would be tremendous.'

'Truly,' said the A.C., 'the soil is good. Show me your gardens, Noha. Baruti, call when the raft is ready.'

They walked through the corn. In some places peanuts and beans were growing in the lush ground and rice gardens flourished near the water's edge.

'Look at that maize and millet,' said Kolongo. 'Look at those peanuts. Probably they're all the harvest you'll get.'

'Words of truth,' agreed Noha, 'unless...' The twittering of weaver birds came from the ripening grain. The bird scarers went into action. Noha shook his head ruefully. 'Your plans for the days ahead are good. But this year we will have famine. The crop is not ripe yet. We can have every man, woman and child of the village chasing those birds, but they still fly down and eat and eat and eat.'

The Area Commissioner nodded slowly. Eagerly Noha continued, 'Monkeys steal corn but the damage they do is nothing when you think of the work of those flying thieves. I have never seen so many. Look at them. Bwana, we must act. Soon our crops will be ripe, then the birds will have a feast and the people's stomachs will be empty.'

They could hear Baruti shouting, 'Ready!'

A sail made from a blanket tied to a bamboo mast was rigged and a length of wood shaped into a steering oar.

After an uncomfortably hot hour the Cooking Pot loomed out of the heat haze. A solid mass of birds rose from inside the crater. For seconds the sun was blotted out. The noise they made was incredible. Then, in a flash, they had passed and were gone.

Kolongo whistled. 'There are myriads of them.'

'Truly, Great One,' agreed Baruti, 'but you have only seen one family of a large tribe.'

Noha brought the raft into the one place where the steep side of the Cooking Pot could be scaled. Soon they were scrambling up, Tembo loaded with pieces of hose, the army sergeant helping Baruti and Noha with the bamboo poles.

The A.C. fanned himself with his hat. 'Let's rest in the shade for a while. Here is water and food.'

Baruti looked pleased. 'That will be a thing of praise. See down there, Bwana A.C., that is where the marijuana grew.'

Tembo ate silently. He very much wanted to make that syphon work. Near to where the raft had drifted was a V-shaped gap in the rim of the crater.

Tembo leaned over and looked at the brown water below him. 'To make this water flow, Bwana Baruti, we will need all the bamboo pipes and every single bit of hose.'

Baruti nodded. 'We must be careful, for if so much as a small mouthful of air enters, then at once the water stops. Let us block anything that even looks like a hole with sticky, milky stuff from the cactus.' The boy agreed, eagerly picking up a tin while Baruti started to dig a narrow pathway for their crude syphon system.

Kolongo and the sergeant stood taking in the broad picture of the problem. Trees, stripped of leaves, were burdened to breaking point with birds' nests, every available twig carrying its tailor-made nest. The tall dry grass and undergrowth were tinder dry.

The A.C. spoke briskly. 'This whole operation needs careful planning. I have arranged for the experts to come and give their ideas.'

'I would suggest, sir, that we measure the area.'

'Right, and we can examine the place while we do so.'

Near to where the raft was moored Baruti, Tembo and Noha were busy pouring water, adjusting hoses and bamboo pipes.

'If it works,' breathed Baruti, 'we have a way of wisdom that will help turn swamp into good land,'

Twice the syphon failed. The third time the pipes were full. There was no leak. Baruti climbed over the edge of the rim and lowered himself until his hand held over the end of the pipe, was under water. He heard a shrill whistle and replied in like fashion. The whistle was repeated. He whipped his hand away from the bottom of the pipe.

A yell of delight came from the far side of the rim. 'It runs! Bwana Baruti, how it runs!'

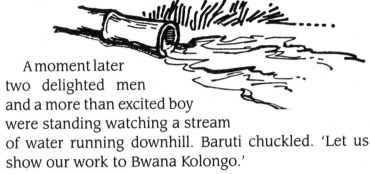

A moment later two delighted men and a more than excited boy were standing watching a stream of water running downhill. Baruti chuckled. 'Let us show our work to Bwana Kolongo.'

As they arrived the A.C. was saying thoughtfully, 'It will take us one and a half hours to cross the swamp. We must...' He stopped. They heard the sound of a small engine across the brown water. Twisting and turning through the reeds was a light metal boat with an outboard motor.

Baruti shaded his eyes. 'It is Yonah Nhuti, the Game Scout, and the Veterinary Officer.'

'This boat will save us an hour,' exclaimed Kolongo. 'He must have brought it down from Lake Victoria.' A moment later he was greeting the new arrivals. He turned to the vet. 'Would you please go around the rim with the sergeant here? He can give you such details as we have worked out so far. And Yonah Nhuti, come with me and we will see the work that has been done in the cave at the bottom of the crater. Bwana Baruti, you lead the way.'

They scrambled down what was now a well-defined track. On one side of it, water was running from a bamboo pipe and creating a small stream.

'Tembo and I thought many thoughts,' said Baruti. 'Dry earth by itself grows nothing and very wet earth which is mud is useless. But if you have water and earth and can mix them in exactly the way you want them, then there is profit and there is food for many people. Behold, down there it looks dark and rumour said it was bottomless but it is not. See,' he took one of the bamboo poles, 'it has perhaps a depth of three metres only, and inside is a long crack. We have blocked more than half of it. We can close off the rest with timber from trees growing in the Pot. Inside the crack this wood will swell when wet and the water that runs down should fill the cave. If concrete is used later on, this could be the water store and the bottom of the swamp could become rice gardens.' He stopped, his eyes flashing.

Kolongo nodded and climbed down the rope into the dark gash. A few minutes later he was back. There was enthusiasm in his voice. 'Baruti, I believe you have the answer. Many details need to be worked out by the engineers, but this broadly is the way to do it.' He moved back up the slope. 'Mmm, good. It's now 3.30 p.m. With this boat we'll be on time. Every minute counts if we are to save this year's harvest.'

Pili Pili had circled the swamp. He shaded his eyes and looked out across the water. Then he stood up and peered at the reeds growing quite close to the edge of the road.

He patted the machine and said gently, 'Punda, clever one, I think you're right. We'll do exactly as you say.' He started the engine again and when a little way past Saba Railway Station he turned the wheel and drove twenty metres beyond the edge of the swamp to a spot where there was the granite boulder the size of an elephant and the shape of an egg sitting on its larger end.

For an hour he scooped stone and shovelled it into the wheel tracks. With satisfaction he inspected a solid track driven well into the reeds. Ahead was the low island Baruti had described. He looked beyond it and shook his head. 'Punda, that will be a place of difficulty. They told me that there is much rock right up to the Cooking Pot. But in between those rocks sometimes mud comes up to a man's middle – thick stuff that eats stone and then perhaps there is really deep water. But of course we can deal with that! Already we have travelled a tenth of the distance in a mere hour. Even with great difficulties surely we can finish the rest of it.' The machine backfired and Pili Pili chuckled.

The engineer drove along in his jeep. He saw the yellow machine working in the reeds and drove down the newly cut road. 'Well, Pepper Pot,' he laughed, 'what are you and your donkey up to? Fishing?'

Pili Pili replied sombrely. 'Bwana Samweli, we fish for birds and we fight famine. Punda here suggested that a small sample of her wisdom might be helpful. When that man with one eye and a mind that works at high speed sees this he will approve. My bones tell me that things are about to happen.'

A voice came from inside the jeep. 'Area Commissioner calling engineer Samuel Mkono. Are your reading me? Over.'

The khaki-dressed figure picked up a microphone, pushed down a switch and answered, 'Mkono to A.C., reading you loud and clear, Mr Kolongo. Over.'

'Will you be at Saba in thirty minutes? Over.'

'I am there now, sir. Over.'

'We need as a matter of urgency to drive a road as near as we can to the place they call the Cooking Pot of Ghosts. Start thinking now. We'll need brisk action. Over and out.'

Pili Pili drummed on the now very muddied side of Punda. He grinned. 'Won't this work give him surprise? We will even see approval in his eye of glass.'

'Stop talking, Pepper Pot, and let's work.'

When, some twenty minutes later, a cloud of dust indicated the coming of the Area Commissioner, not only was there a sizeable sample of road made but there were plans on paper. When these had been carefully looked into, Pili Pili summed up the situation, 'Punda has much confidence.'

Nelson Kolongo stood at the end of the table. 'It is 4.30. Thank you for being here on time. Now, I welcome you, representing as you do the Army, the Veterinary, Agriculture and the Public Works Departments. We have also a number of citizens of Tanzania who have helped us. Considerable thought has gone into the idea of turning this swamp into a fine food-producing area. In working on this project we have met a complication. A new enemy to our crops has appeared in the shape of millions of weaver birds. They can do tremendous damage. I have a memorandum regarding their activities on the other side of the continent in Senegal. Fifty million of them attacked the rice crop there, eating enough food each day for two hundred thousand people. We have to do something about them here. Each bird lives seven years. Each pair produces two or three young ones in a brood in those attractive nests that they build. They are a formidable enemy. How shall we plan battle?'

'We must work fast,' said the agricultural officer. 'The crops will be ripe in three weeks and these food thieves will be at it before then, and weaver birds are capable of attacking crops up to three hundred miles away.'

As he finished speaking, the Army man stood up holding a folder. 'Exactly what to do is drawn up here. We can organise the attack if it is possible to put our men and material on the spot. These birds are cunning. They pick places that are hard to reach and where there are snakes and crocodiles. Get us on the spot and we will be ready in ten days – a week for the materials to reach Saba and three days to prepare on the island.'

The engineer spoke. 'Bwana A.C., we can build that road. It is nearly the time of sundown. I suggest that you come and see what has already been done in a matter of hours.'

The A.C. nodded. 'Let me sum up then. This Cooking Pot is the main target. It is alive with weaver birds. Its trees are weighed down with their nests. We know our enemy. We know our battle ground. Now to find the time to attack. Let us go and look at this road and see how the birds behave at this time of the day.'

They were within a hundred metres of the place where Punda had ploughed into the soft mud when suddenly the sky seemed alive with beating wings. Some of the birds peeled off to land in the reeds but the vast majority swept on. Over the Cooking Pot they massed together and dropped from the sky like a thunder shower. Three times from different directions a similar thing happened. The sun was moving over the horizon.

Kolongo turned on his heel. 'That place is the volcano from which a famine can erupt. The fight is on and the question is, who will eat this harvest, man or bird?'

13

Nightmare

In the shade of his jeep squatted the District Engineer and Pili Pili. 'Punda is weary,' said the latter. 'All day she has scooped earth with her nose, carried stones with her teeth and dug with strength with her back legs.'

'And in two days' time,' said Samuel Mkono the engineer, 'they want to take hundreds of gallons of fluid that burns with speed and heat into the Cooking Pot. It will be in forty-four gallon drums. This will be no simple matter. They will wire the place so that when the plunger is pushed the dynamite will blow up the enemy. There will be great fire and destruction.'

'Punda and I have no joy in this part of the work,' said Pili Pili. 'These small birds are food for the eyes. They build with skill. They do no harm.'

The engineer grunted. 'Open your eyes, Pepper Pot. They fly in great tribes over hundreds of miles of our country and eat the food of millions of our people. They may even invade Kenya and Zaire and Malawi from this spot. If that Cooking Pot stays filled with hungry birds, children will go hungry, the strength of many will become small, disease will conquer the old and the weak, and all will know the bitterness of famine. Do we not both remember the days of the coming of the grasshoppers?'

Pili Pili jumped to his feet. 'Your mouth is suddenly full of words. I understand very well what you say but still I draw back from this killing and the way you plan to do it.'

Mkono shrugged. 'Why not suggest some other way? Who is to die? People or birds? In our plan, small birds will die in the time that it takes to strike a match. Their end comes with great suddenness. Not so is the way of poison.'

As they moved off Samuel Mkono said, 'If we found a way to drive them from this place then they would only destroy the crop somewhere else. Suppose we drove them out to sea? Their death would then be long and cruel.'

Pili Pili drove the jeep in silence to the game scout's house. Here, as he stopped for the engineer to get down, he sighed, 'My heart is heavy. There will be no singing on this safari.'

In the half light he drove to where the large yellow machine towered above the reeds. He slapped the rear wheel. 'Oh my Punda, in two days we've worked hard and well. Rest while I collect the device shaped like a giraffe's neck which we use to drag out reeds.'

He jumped into the jeep and drove on around the swamp. Dozens of times, dense clouds of weaver birds flew overhead. Pili Pili groaned. 'Why are there so many of you? Even today, if each of you has filled your stomachs with but ten grains of millet many a harvest and many a family will suffer. You weave with skill, but when you and your many relations descend like a hailstorm upon the crops we must defend them. We do it with sadness, but do it we must.'

He thought of the three nests in the tree at the P.W.D. camp. The cheeky, friendly little birds had learned to fly down and eat grain from his hand. Never once had they regarded ten grains as even the beginning of a meal.

It grew darker. Frogs and crickets started their nightly duet. Mosquitoes found their way into the jeep. 'Small birds,' muttered Pili Pili, 'why don't you change your ideas about food? Eat mosquitoes, not grain.'

Trees started to meet overhead. He saw the turn-off to Nungho and Furahi. A deep pothole loomed up ahead. He pushed hard on the brake and swung the wheel. The headlights showed up a hyaena, its eyes fixed on something in the shadows. Pili Pili tooted his horn and the hyaena shambled off while the lights showed a body lying beside the road. He stopped with a jerk, jumped down and looked at the unconscious man.

Pili Pili rolled his eyes. 'It is Bwana Penicillin himself.' He bent over the ragged figure and gently touched his

111

bruised and swollen face. 'Truly, your paths have led you into peril today.'

Half an hour later, Pili Pili gently lowered Yakobo onto a sleeping mat in the shed that normally housed Punda. He wrapped him in a blanket, sponged his face and then walked across to the kitchen to make tea. As he boiled the water, a wild-eyed figure staggered towards him.

'They would kill me. They...' gasped Yakobo. He found himself looking into a smiling face.

'There is no need to fear. It is I, Pili Pili, who makes roads.' Two strong hands guided the dazed man to a stool.

'Lugu seeks my death,' muttered Yakobo. 'He and Dolla have taken everything I had and now they would murder me.'

Pili Pili handed him a cup of tea. There was a chuckle in his voice. 'They've had small success so far. Your life is still within your skin. Take courage and drink this.'

'They must not know I am here.' Yakobo slumped onto the stool spilling half of the pot of tea.

'I shall not tell them,' said Pili Pili as he walked to another shed to collect the equipment he needed. He lashed it to the roof of the jeep. As he was tying the last knot, Yakobo walked up looking more like himself.

Huskily he said, 'My wisdom is small because they hit me on the head with a chair. My life is in danger in this place. I must hide.'

Pili Pili grinned. 'Who is to know? Rest and regain strength. The door of Punda's house has a lock that shuts itself. Keep out of sight and make no noise and you will be safe.' He walked with Yakobo to the spacious shed, switched on his torch and pointed to a large gourd and a box. 'See, here is water and food.' He wrapped the blanket round Yakobo. 'Goodbye. And do not forget that when the lock clicks the door is shut.'

Yakobo watched the headlights disappear. Loneliness seemed to close in on him. His head throbbed and his whole body ached. He knew this was malaria. As he lay there in misery he cursed himself for leaving the hospital.

At last he fell into a fitful sleep. He seemed to be back in the ward in his white uniform, holding up a card and saying, 'If sinners entice...' Dolla was coming towards him. With every step his fine clothes seemed to change colour. Out of the shadows came Lugu holding a bag of money. He swung it viciously. Agonising pain shot through Yakobo's head. With a scream he sat up. His teeth were chattering. He felt terribly cold. He pulled the blanket over his head and slept again.

Again Yakobo dreamed. Lugu's voice seemed to chuckle, 'No escape. No escape.' A book opened in front of him. He could see the words, 'How shall we escape if we neglect such a great salvation?' How would he escape? How? Neglect? He had done much more than neglect.

Yakobo woke with a start. There was the sound of cattle being driven to pasture. Light came in through the window. Who sent these words running through his brain! 'I will get up and go to my father and say,

"Father, I have sinned against both God and you. I'm not fit to be called your son any longer."' He set his teeth. He was no prodigal son. He wasn't without money. He wouldn't eat pig food. If he'd sinned, what of it? He could look after himself. Why all this running away, this hiding? He felt much better. It was the fever that did this to him. Who took any notice of dreams? He lay back and slept once again.

14
Eaten by Ants

The sun was well over the hills. Pili Pili had been at work already for two hours. He was singing a song of encouragement which blended with the sound of Punda's motor. The long attachment that he had brought the night before was scooping out clumps of reeds. The machine moved forward a metre and again scooped a dripping mass of stalks and mud from the side of the long stretch of granite.

At midday Pili Pili stopped Punda's motor and said, 'Donkey, never has a morning gone faster. You have worked with high skill. Half the day over and a day's work done. They demanded that we should finish the road to this place. It is done. They demanded that by this time tomorrow the reeds should be cleared out so that rafts might come up to that sloping piece of rock. We will do it.'

He watched a train arrive and two trucks being shunted off. One was full of oil drums. The other was bright red and had the word EXPLOSIVES written across it. Overhead flew an aeroplane. 'It flies to the hospital,' thought Pili Pili and gave Punda a wordy discourse on flying. He had barely finished when the plane circled the hospital thirty kilometres away and came in to land on the airstrip.

There Dr Matama hurried forward to greet the pilot who shook hands. 'I have a letter for you from the A.C. He says I must have you on the Saba airstrip two hours before sunset.'

Daudi tore open the envelope and read, 'Request you come to Saba with medical supplies for any casualty in the battle against the birds. Kolongo A.C.'

In mid-afternoon the whole country seemed alive with weaver birds. They disturbed Yakobo as he lay muttering in delirium. They flew chattering over Baruti and Noha, who were inspecting two rafts which would ferry the fire liquid and explosives to the Cooking Pot.

The sky was full of birds from the moment the plane took off from the hospital.

'We could be in trouble,' shouted the pilot as a wave of weaver birds swung towards the aeroplane. There was a loud thump and the cabin was suddenly dark. The aircraft shuddered. The engine faltered, spluttered and then picked up. The pilot grunted. 'That was close.' He turned on the windscreen wipers and an ugly mess of blood and feathers was scraped aside to give him a view of the landing strip.

Below them Nelson Kolongo turned to Yonah. 'The people will come to hear my words?'

Yonah nodded. 'Every village within ten kilometres has heard but none will come till after dark. Everybody, young and old is guarding the crops. They see more and more young birds among those that would steal their grain.'

'This is the time to talk with them.'

'Truly, Bwana A.C., we have also arranged for three goats to be killed. Even now they are stewing them. The people will forget some of their anger and will dance. A full stomach and some dancing will do much to cover up their worry.'

'There should be time to see all our preparations on this side of the swamp before sunset,' said Nelson Kolongo, 'and tomorrow we'll visit the Cooking Pot.' He had a warm feeling of satisfaction, for all the plans had gone like clockwork.

The trim little plane landed and taxied towards them. It looked as though it had been covered with tar and then sprayed with feathers. The pilot and Daudi Matama swung down to the ground.

After the usual greetings Daudi Matama said, 'We nearly didn't arrive. The sky was full of birds.'

'I am glad all is well,' said Nelson Kolongo. 'This is certainly a danger spot. The crops ripen early. We've timed our attack well.'

'I must leave you to it,' said the pilot, waving goodbye.

They watched the plane move off, rise into the air and disappear over the hills.

Nelson Kolongo led the way to the Land Rover. Soon they bumped past Yonah Nhuti's house and the railway station and turned into the swamp at the egg-shaped boulder.

The A.C. pointed ahead. 'Pili Pili has done well in building this road. At the moment he is deepening a waterway to carry rafts with the materials we need for this battle.' They were driving deep into the swamp. From the reeds which grew some two metres above the surface dangled hundreds of nests, and every minute more and more weaver birds swirled down.

'A well-planned road this,' said Daudi. 'There is wisdom in the way you have linked up those flat stony places.'

Kolongo nodded. 'Pili Pili has made a solid entry to within a stone's throw of the Cooking Pot.'

The engineer hurried out of the reeds. 'Good evening, Dr Matama.' He grinned at Tembo and Baruti. 'I would like to report that the work is finished.'

'Well done,' said the A.C. 'And now for the enemy.'

'Every day more and more of them come,' said Baruti.

Dr Daudi pointed to the hills to the south. 'Over there we hear the same thing. Very few people are coming to the hospital. Everybody is out bird-scaring.'

In the starlight a crowd of people stood outside Yonah's house.

A loud voice shouted, 'Our crops are in danger!'

Yonah stood up and cleared his throat. 'Bwana Kolongo, these small birds are coming in great numbers to every village and every garden. The young are now flying with the old. The crops ripen, in some places they are ripe and these feathered thieves steal even from the baskets on the women's heads.'

'Shoot them!' shouted a voice. 'Give us guns and bullets.'

A roar of agreement greeted this.

'What is all this that you do with roads and soldiers?' demanded another.

Kolongo stood up. 'This harvest will be saved. There are millions of those birds. There are those who shoot them with catapults. It is useless. Guns are no better.' A thousand *askaris* with a thousand guns would not begin to halt them. We have traced the great nest from which they come. It is the Cooking Pot.'

There was an excited murmur. 'Is it a matter of witchcraft? That is a forbidden place.'

'Have no worry,' said Kolongo. 'But in this battle we fight with fire and we shall win. All of you keep away from the road to the Cooking Pot and the swamp. Keep out of the way of those that fight.'

For half an hour he answered questions. Then people started clapping their hands and dancing.

Yakobo was still weak with fever and from the beating he had received. He clutched Pili Pili's jungle knife and stood in front of the baobab tree where he'd hidden his money. He stumbled around to the far side where no car headlights would betray him. In the gloom he started to chop. After a dozen strokes he dropped the great knife and leaned panting against the tree. After a while he pulled oil-soaked cotton waste from his pocket and lit a handful. By its light he chopped purposefully. Fatigue came over him in waves but he hacked on. The flame flickered and went out as the blade cut into the hollow of the buyu tree.

In complete darkness Yakobo squatted on a gnarled root fighting for breath. Thoughts raced through his mind. Why had he ever come on this safari? His mind went back over the years to the days when he'd first met Dolla and seen those magnificent clothes. Up till then his hospital work had had something special about it – watching people brought back from the brink of death.

He staggered to his feet. It was money that had attracted him. His money was in that tree in front of him. He hacked away until he had made a sizeable hole in the tree before he needed to rest again.

Yakobo tore what was left of the cotton waste in half, lighted it and in a frenzy slashed at the hole. Five minutes later he was crawling into the darkness of the trunk. Deliberately, to taste the full flavour of his success, he stopped, arranged the last of his oily rag and struck a match.

The inside of the venerable tree was an odd pattern of termite tracks. His foot kicked a piece of dead branch which was riddled with white ants. There were the rubber bands and string that had held his roll of notes together. Around them was a handful of powdery mud and some scraps of engraved paper. With hands that trembled he picked these up. They were fragments of East African bank notes. Wildly he clawed about in the rubbish on the floor. The flame flickered and went out. Then with a groan he crawled back into the night. There was a horrible emptiness in his stomach. Everything he had was gone.

Again words echoed in his memory, 'Where moths

and rust spoil and where thieves break through and steal. Where your riches are you may be certain that your heart will be there too.' He spat. 'Riches!' The voice spoke again in his head. 'You cannot serve two masters. You cannot serve God and money. You shall not covet,' rang out in his ears like the blows of the *panga* into the tree trunk against which he leaned.

'Covet.' He had asked Daudi Matama to explain that and he knew what it meant. 'Why shouldn't I have what he has? It had all started with Dolla's first visit, but it could have stopped there if he had wanted it to. But how often had his mind told him, 'I must have this. I must have that.'

He thought of things. He thought of people. Only a week ago he had had within his grasp everything that he had dreamed of wanting. But now his hands were empty. His clothes were strips of rag. His feet were bare. With a groan he stumbled back to the Public Works Department camp. He would throw himself down on that mat and sleep. If only sleep would take him right out of life itself! Misery. Hopelessness. Despair. These were his only possessions. He reached the door and pushed it. It was locked. He hadn't remembered to prop it open and the wind had slammed it.

'A fool,' he muttered. 'I've been worse than a fool.' Dejectedly he walked out into the night.

At sunset, back at Nungho, Lugu put down his cup. The agile way he had slipped the powder from the sleeping capsules into Hamisi's coffee pleased him.

The Arab yawned. 'Must be in for an attack of fever,' he muttered.

121

Ten minutes later Lugu heard him snoring. Now to let off the lorry's handbrake! With satisfaction Lugu watched the big vehicle start rolling downhill towards the swamp.

He woke Dolla and chuckled. 'My end of the work goes surprisingly well. The lorry is here. The wind blows in the right direction. Nyale is drunk but his fires burn, distilling his powerful honey drink. You now go down to within sight of the huge mango tree on the swamp edge. There are those that guard their riches but watchfulness will disappear when the fire starts. When you see flames eating Nyale's house, walk out seven paces into the swamp and your feet will tell you where the ivory is. Drag it to dry land and I will meet you with the machine. Any questions?'

Dolla spat. 'I hate mud.'

Lugu's voice was soft. 'But you love money. Now get going.' He rattled a box of matches and disappeared into the gloom.

Dolla took off his shoes and socks and rolled up his trousers. His thoughts were centred on how to keep those six elephant tusks for himself. Plan after plan moved through his head. Suddenly the darkness was cut open not far to his right. Flames leapt up. There were some muffled explosions and the wind swept the blaze through the timber, earth and grass-thatched roof. He heard shouting and watched running figures.

Quickly Dolla walked into the mud. It sucked at his legs and water splashed up into his face. He cursed softly but was silent when his feet touched ivory. With difficulty he dragged tusk after tusk to the bank. Muttering, he struggled with the sixth as the lorry, without its headlights, stopped half under the tree.

Lugu's voice came smoothly. 'Efficient work indeed. I see you have the ivory.'

Almost silently they loaded the lorry and Lugu drove quietly toward the P.W.D. camp. They bundled the elephants' tusks into hessian bags and hid them under a pile of rusting iron sheeting.

As they drove back to Nungho, Lugu chuckled, 'Congratulations, Bwana Dolla. In three days a certain person will pick those up and we will each be richer by a thousand shillings.'

Dolla grunted. 'I will need to be. From the ribs down I am soaking wet. Mud, filthy mud, clings to me. If am seen like this it will be but a short journey to jail.'

'Peace,' murmured Lugu. 'Did you see the fine natural way that fire started and spread? Nyale was suitably drunk. The place where he distilled was carelessly arranged. It was a simple matter for the fire water that he was making to burst into flame. The wind played its part admirably.' He stopped opposite the room where Yakobo had lived.

'Bwana Dolla, I am always thinking of you.' He pushed into the shivering man's hands a gourd of mead. 'Rest here while I return the lorry, but leave a little for me.'

Again Dolla grunted but as soon as Lugu had driven off he started to drink greedily.

Most of the people of the village had gone to look at the smouldering ruins of Nyale's house. Down the road, its headlights blazing, came a police jeep. Lugu quietly closed the lorry door and, keeping always in the shadow, hurried back to Yakobo's room.

Dolla had upset the gourd of mead and lay flat on his back breathing heavily. Lugu produced from his pocket a sawn-off portion of rhino horn and place it in Dolla's pocket. Then he rolled the drunken man over, pulled up his shirt and wrenched from between his shoulder blades a plastic bag filled with notes.

'Lovely money,' whispered Lugu. 'You won't be needing that where you'll be when you wake up.' He lit a candle and with his left hand printed in wobbly letters, 'The man you are looking for is in the place where medicine was once injected. Also Arabs buy much ivory these days.' This note he placed on the front of the police jeep.

Gripping the green suitcase with its contents of marijuana and bank notes, he murmured to himself, 'Winston Churchill Lugu, you are in excellent form.' He stopped, looked warily around and then raised the canvas cover of the trailer attached to the police jeep. It was empty. Boldly he placed the suitcase inside, stepped in himself, clipped the cover back in place and lay quietly on the floor.

Time went by. From where Lugu lay he heard voices and the crackle of the radio phone. He smiled as a very drunk Dolla was pushed into the jeep and they moved off. It was more than uncomfortable as the trailer bumped about over the rough road.

At last they stopped. Lugu heard Kolongo's voice.

'Well done. You have him safely?'

'Yes, Bwana A.C. It is only a pity we couldn't find the money.'

'It's there,' chuckled the Area Commissioner. 'Why do you think I insisted on the trailer being attached? It was more than Dolla's partner could resist, to escape with the loot by the courtesy of the police.'

The cover was wrenched off the trailer and, for once in his career, Lugu was speechless.

In the house of Yonah the Game Scout an alarm clock went off an hour before sunrise, waking all the officials.

Over breakfast a quarter of an hour later Nelson Kolongo said, 'Today is going to be long and exacting. Here is the program. Report half an hour after first light on the condition of the road and waterway to the Cooking Pot. If these are still satisfactory, I will give the all-clear to the army to unload the drums of fire fluid and the dynamite from the railway trucks and they will take it out by lorry to the long strip of granite where they will be loaded onto the rafts and then taken into the Cooking Pot itself.' He drew a deep breath. 'We will be there to see this happen. The army say they want four hours at least to fix their fire bombs after the fuel drums and the explosives are landed.'

15

Potful of Flame

'Come over to the Cooking Pot,' said Nelson Kolongo to Dr Matama.

Soon they were moving across the water and climbing the steps up the side of the crater. At the top, beaming down, was the engineer.

'You will be interested in his explanation as to how he has followed up Baruti's mending of this cracked Pot,' smiled Kolongo. 'He's ready to start at dawn tomorrow pouring cement and running a pump.'

The doctor gripped the engineer's hand. 'Samweli Mkono, it's good to see you. We…ouch!'

Into their faces flew fluttering, chattering birds.

'Head down and arms up and they won't worry you much,' shouted Samuel Mkono as they clambered down towards the bottom of the crater. Nests bounced and bumped against them, bringing screaming protests from the brown balls of feathers that had woven them.

'This Pot boils with birds,' shouted Daudi Matama, to make himself heard above the din.

'Gets even better when you're down near our workings,' boomed Mkono. He gripped the arm of Baruti who had just joined them. 'That was a first-rate idea of yours. All we've done is to put in a stronger plug and we'll use a pump instead of a syphon. As soon as we've finished fighting birds, I'll start a battle against mud.'

'And,' nodded Daudi Matama, 'the Agricultural Officer thinks that, with irrigation, gardens here could produce two crops a year.'

Baruti had a broad smile. 'Come, let us look at the other parts of the Pot.'

They climbed back up the steep hill. Half way, weaver birds erupted in pandemonium. The A.C. hurried towards them shouting. 'See those white pegs? This is where the tins of fire fluid will be placed.'

Over the rim of the crater appeared soldiers pushing one of the large red drums. It was rolled into place.

Kolongo called his team together. 'All should go as planned. I shall be on the granite island half way down the road. Those who have completed their work, relax in the heat of the day. It is nearly 11 a.m. I want reports each hour. Let us return to base.'

Baruti saw him returning. 'Here comes the A.C. looking stormy.'

'Tea is good medicine for that,' laughed the doctor.

Nelson Kolongo sat down with them in the shade and drank cup after cup of tea as the sun climbed higher.

In the heat haze three kilometres away, Yakobo, feeling utterly lonely and wretched, walked unsteadily to a baobab tree and sank between two roots. He was weak with hunger and thirst. The sun beat down.

A cheerful voice greeted him. 'Bwana Yakobo. What news?'

'The news is good,' he mumbled, peering up at an extremely tall, smiling young man.

'Do you not remember me at the hospital?'

Yakobo shrugged and turned his head away.

'Did they not build a new bed with six legs,' chuckled the tall man, 'two at each end and two in the middle?'

Yakobo grunted.

'I'm glad you remember. I am Mfupi, the short one, so called because I am so long. Life was going from within my skin when I reached the hospital and you looked after me. You were the one who gave me injections.'

'Oh, shut up about injections. Shut up about the hospital,' snapped Yakobo, trying to move away.

'Truly,' said Mfupi, 'the strength has gone from your body. The house of my brother is near. Come and eat food.'

'Clear out,' growled Yakobo, closing his eyes.

Mfupi walked away silently. Twenty minutes later he was back with food and a gourd full of cold water. Yakobo took it and drank deeply.

'Eat a small amount,' urged Mfupi, squatting down.

Reluctantly Yakobo did so. Soon it started to do him good. A look of satisfaction spread over Mfupi's face.

'When I came to the hospital, death was close and all was hopelessness. But you came with kindness and talked to me. You told me of the man with two sons. The elder had wisdom in the matter of cattle and gardens, but the younger wished to travel to see what goes on beyond the hills. He talked many words. His father agreed to divide his wealth between his sons. The young man set out on his safari and he enjoyed himself. Perhaps he traded well, perhaps he made money, but he'd learnt to spend as well. The day came when his pocket was empty, his stomach also.'

Mfupi saw that bowl of food was nearly empty. He put six bananas beside Yakobo, who looked up at him. 'The boy you spoke of did not have food such as you have given me, but rather of the sort prepared for pigs.'

Yakobo sighed. 'I remember those times. My heart was warm as we talked together about Jesus. But that's all over now. I chose to walk in darkness. When sinners enticed me, I listened to them and I travelled their ways. Truly, those are ways that end in death.' He shuddered. 'I am condemned.'

'I know the verse,' said Mfupi: '"This is the judgment that has come into the world that men love darkness rather than light because their deeds were evil." Could it be that your love of darkness is not what it was? Truly, you turned your back on me and you didn't deserve your food.' Yakobo looked up sharply but Mfupi was smiling. 'It made my heart warm to bring it and talk to you and I am only Mfupi, a man. God is so different. He will forgive. Think of these things while you rest. Here is a blanket.'

Yakobo leaned back against the tree and closed his eyes.

Mfupi watched flight after flight of birds. Many of them seemed to be coming over the hills. A multitude of wings flashed in the sunlight. In the distance he could see lorries on the road that led to the Cooking Pot. Near the station was the red van and the yellow of Pili Pili's machine. Up the hills were the deep greens of the thornbush and nearer the brown water were tawny stretches of dried grass.

He thought, 'One day snakes and mosquitoes and the creatures that cause disease and annoyance will be gone. Water will run obediently to the places where it is needed. Mud will become soil which will produce fine crops.'

Mfupi looked at the sleeping man whose face was bruised and haggard and dirty. He had often prayed for Yakobo and, in these last months, urgently, though he knew that Yakobo hadn't thought of him for years.

At six o'clock the sun was setting. A wind blew across the swamp. With it came birds and birds and still more birds.

Yakobo's eyes opened. 'Those clouds – are they not red?'

Mfupi sat beside him. 'You used to say that to me as we looked through the hospital window and then…'

'I remember,' said Yakobo. '"Though your sins be as scarlet they shall be as white as snow. Though they be red like crimson they shall be as wool."'

'That's what happened to mine,' nodded his companion.

Yakobo struggled to his feet. 'I have been a fool.'

'Yes,' encouraged Mfupi, 'and what's the next step?'

'I will go to my father and I will say, "Father, I have sinned against heaven and before you and I am no longer worthy to be called your son."' Yakobo's voice faded into silence.

'It is a thing of great worth for a man to become a son of God. And even though his wickedness be large and his foolishness vast, how can he cease to be a son?'

He put his hand on Yakobo's shoulder and led the way. Mirrored in the water, the sunset looked blood-red.

The radio phone buzzed. 'Sergeant Mapinde reporting from Cooking Pot. Time 18.00. Everything ready, Bwana A.C. Flame-throwers in position for follow-up to main explosion. Over and out.'

'Thank you. Over and out,' said Kolongo.

'We're ready to destroy,' said Daudi Matama quietly, 'but what about repairing? Do you think we may still salvage Yakobo?'

'Don't talk to me about him,' snapped Kolongo. 'There is something I want you to understand very clearly. This Yakobo is a hypocrite – preaching, reading the Bible, going to church, and then being thoroughly dishonest, capping it off by stealing syringes and medicines and starting a penicillin racket.' He looked up sharply. 'How much did he steal?'

'Oh, about twelve hundred shilling worth.'

'I thought it would be more. If he shows up I'll put him under arrest. I know you think differently. He's been your helper and friend for years at the hospital. If you came across him surely he wouldn't be reinstated without penalty?'

'If he was still determined to go his own way and money was his master, no. But if he changed his mind about the way he was living and Jesus Christ was again his Commanding Officer, I think he'd be taken back, but he would lose seniority.'

'Would you expect him to make restitution?'

'Of course. His repentance wouldn't be real unless he paid back what he owed. What are his other debts?'

'Close to a thousand shillings.'

'If you jail him, how can he pay that back?'

'It would teach him a lesson and he'd be a solid warning to many young men doing the same sort of work.'

'But if he paid up or the people he owed money to forgave him, or somebody paid for him, what then?'

'He's still guilty.'

'If you were in his boots how would you feel?'

Kolongo answered with a wry smile. 'You hospital people are all the same. You're back again to the "little sins that do the damage". I've been thinking this over. Yes, I'm full of pride. And I'll tell a lie or two if it's going to…'

'And, of course, the worst sin of all is turning your back on God.'

'Oh, yes, I'm guilty of that. But one day I'll start thinking differently – when it's convenient, when I have time.'

A shadow raced towards them. 'Birds,' said the A.C. 'The place is thick with them. They're guilty and they'll perish.'

Daudi nodded. 'We don't like condemning them. But as you have said, there are more important things. In your own life, though, you sidestep these vital matters. Although you see the urgency of saving harvest and improving pastures and irrigation…'

Kolongo held up his hand. 'Enough, stop!'

'Have it your own way,' said the doctor.

'I will,' snapped Kolongo. 'Yakobo's a thief and must pay for his thieving. He's guilty. It isn't that I like punishing, but you can't steal and get away with it any more than I can be soft-hearted about those birds.' He looked at the crimson sunset and sighed. 'And now I must carry through the sentence on these grain thieves.'

Darkness fell. A musty smell drifted in from the swamp. Above them came the whir of the wings of an army of weaver birds.

'18.30 hours,' said the A.C. 'A crowd is gathering.' He picked up his radio phone. 'Kolongo speaking. Sergeant, is all in order? Over.'

'Completely, sir. Over.'

'Good. We'll come and join you at the Cooking Pot end of the road. Next communication will be at 18.55. The explosion is timed for 19.00 hours. Over and out.'

'Corporal Juma,' he called. 'Set up a barrier where the road narrows and allow no one to pass beyond.'

An uneasy stillness hovered over the swamp. Nearby was the sound of excited conversation from the crowd on the road.

Nelson Kolongo spoke crisply through the amplifiers. 'This is the Area Commissioner. In two minutes' time we shall kill by fire and explosive millions of birds that have been raiding our crops and who would plunder the harvest of the four million people who live within their flight range. Your government with the men of the army, the veterinary, the agricultural and the public works departments have prepared for weeks for what is about to happen. Remember, famine fighting is not without risks. Behave calmly. Beware of fire and flying sparks.' He looked round and said, 'Action.'

A huge hand reached for the microphone and the sergeant's voice boomed through the darkness. 'Flame-throwers. Alert.'

'I shall count from ten to one. On the count of one the explosion will occur. Ready everybody?'

'Ready,' came a hushed chorus.

He started to count, 'Ten, nine, eight, seven, six, five, four, three, two, one.' He rammed down the plunger.

Dazzling light burst from the Cooking Pot. The countryside rocked with the thunder of the explosion. The dynamite blasted the drums of fire fluid. A blazing pillar rocketed high into the air. Sheets of flames spewed in all directions. For a terrifying moment everything was dyed eerie crimson, then a scorching surge of heat swept out from the crater. In a searing but merciful second the execution was over. Every bird on that island had been wiped out and every nest turned to ashes. Sparks and burning twigs rained down. Among the reeds fires started and from six separate places flame-throwers started to belch fire. Between the Cooking Pot and the railway, leaping flames writhed and twisted. Trees laden with nests turned into torches. Children screamed and men and women put their hands over their eyes to shield them from the glare and the smoke.

Nelson Kolongo spoke with conviction. 'It is terrifying but absolutely necessary.'

The fires were dying down. The men with flame-throwers moved along winding channels that had been hidden by the reeds, burning any patches that had escaped. The swamp glowed with a million pinpoints of light. And then the drums started to beat and the people began to sing and dance.

Nelson Kolongo walked from group to group. 'Sergeant, yours was work well done. You and your men will receive special mention in my report. Pili Pili, we would never have been able to do this without your skill and enthusiasm.'

A voice replied through the darkness. 'Thank you. Punda would have had joy in what you are saying but these sparks can be trying to one as sensitive as she is.'

The A.C. gripped Baruti's hand, then Noha's, and put his arm around Tembo. 'You men have done more for your country than you know. The spirit that you have shown we must indeed cultivate among the people of Tanzania.'

16
Out of the Swamp

Mboga had arrived in the hospital Land Rover.

Tembo was filling the radiator. 'My memory is filled with last night,' he said. 'Silence and darkness and whispering. Then loud noises, explosion and a sky full of flame, sparks and smoke.'

'It will look different in daylight,' said Daudi. 'Let's go and see.'

Many other people were walking down Pili Pili's road looking at the five kilometre stretch of grey and black ash that the day before had been matted reeds and undergrowth and thornbush. The morning air was heavy with smoke.

The Land Rover turned in at the egg-shaped boulder, stopping on the first wide stretch of granite.

Ahead of them were two men looking over the brown water. One was exceptionally tall, the other, though his clothes were in tatters, they recognised at once.

Dr Matama hurried forward calling, 'Yakobo! It's good to see you.' He stretched out his hand. Yakobo hesitated and then their hands gripped.

The other joined them, obviously delighted to see Yakobo. Mboga chuckled. 'Is it not Mfupi, the man with the largest bed and the loudest cough in the hospital?'

There was a strange silence. There was no sound of weaver birds, no noise of wind through the reeds.

They walked quite a way towards the Cooking Pot before Baruti said, 'Yakobo, we heard that you had made a lot of money.'

Yakobo pushed a stone around with his bare toes. 'I lost it all. I have lost everything.'

'Not everything,' said Dr Daudi.

Yakobo looked at them with a twisted smile. In a tired voice he said, 'Truly, I have travelled the ways of small wisdom.' He looked out over the drab, scorched fringe of the swamp. 'Everything is gone.'

The young doctor nodded. 'But everything had to go to save the harvest.'

Yakobo's head jerked up.

'That harvest,' went on Daudi, pointing with his chin towards the green of millet and maize gardens. He looked squarely at Yakobo. 'And the one you can produce for God.'

'It's too late,' murmured Yakobo. 'Don't you understand? I've broken commandment after commandment. I've gone too far. Too far.'

'That's strange,' said Daudi. 'Has your memory lost its strength?'

Yakobo threw a pebble into the water. 'My memory has plagued me. Verses from the Bible force their way into my mind. It has been as though a voice has spoken day after day. I've closed my ears to it and tried to keep from taking notice. But at night and in my dreams I could not escape it.'

A soft chuckle came from Baruti. 'Our prayers have kept your conscience alive. Remember the verse that says, "I have blotted out as a thick cloud your transgressions and as a cloud your sins. Return to me for I have brought you back."'

Daudi nodded. 'You may have turned your back on God, you may have travelled away from him, but that doesn't mean you have ceased to be his son. Do you remember that night under the baobab tree near the gate of the hospital? You read me words from God's book, "As many as received Jesus and invited him into their hearts to them he gave the power and authority to become children of God, to as many of them as believed on his name."'

Yakobo nodded.

'You became a son of God that day. You had no doubt about it?'

'I had no doubt then.'

'And now your heart calls for him. When that happens you can be sure, tremendously sure, that he is still your Father and you are still his son. But you have to ask him to forgive you and it is your responsibility to make right anything that you have done wrong to others.'

Yakobo flinched. 'Indeed I have much work to do in this matter.' He sighed and looked away again.

Urgently from further up the road came the distress signal. A frantic woman was wringing her hands and screaming.

'What's happened?' shouted Baruti.

'My child! He's fallen into the water. He will drown!'

Yakobo shouted. 'Where? Where did he fall in?'

She pointed with her chin.

Yakobo did not hesitate. He dived into the muddy water. The water settled quietly. It seemed that he must be tangled in weed or snagged in an underwater bush.

'Will he never come up again?' exploded Mboga.

As if in answer Yakobo came to the surface, shook the water out of his eyes, took a deep breath and dived again.

Dr Matama's eyes were on his watch. 'Thirty seconds. Forty-five.' He was about to say, sixty, when Yakobo appeared grasping the arm of a completely limp boy.'

'My son!' screamed the woman. 'Give him to me!'

Baruti barred her way and said, 'Go gently. Dr Matama can save your child.'

Gasping, Yakobo laid the child down.

'This is the way,' said Mboga. 'Face to one side, feet higher than head!'

Water drained from the lax mouth. Dr Daudi's hand was over the child's heart. 'It's beating but not very strongly. I'll do mouth-to-mouth treatment for five minutes then you take over, Yakobo.'

He held the child's nose and breathed gently and rhythmically into the boy's chest.

People crowded round. The mother shrieked. 'He's dead! My child's dead!' She threw herself at Baruti.

'He'll live,' panted Yakobo, 'if we work with wisdom.'

The mother rolled her eyes wildly and started the death wail. Other women joined in. Men came running up and started to argue. The wall of legs that surrounded the hospital team shuffled closer.

Yakobo touched the doctor on the shoulder. 'Five minutes,' he muttered, taking over.

The temper of the crowd was growing ugly. The women's voices became frenzied. Time dragged.

Yakobo had been resuscitating for some minutes when an old man shouted harshly, 'What evil thing are they doing? What witchcraft is this?'

The death chant was stirring the crowd into hysteria.

'Give me a spear!' shouted a husky voice.

Mboga urged, 'Let me do it for a while.'

Daudi Matama nodded and Yakobo stood up gasping. Baruti held up his hand. 'Quiet! This is the new way...'

'The child is dead!' shouted a man moving purposefully towards Mboga with a knobbed stick. He swung it high but Yakobo grasped it from behind. The man's shouting stopped in his throat as the boy sneezed and started to breathe again.

The people stood back thunderstruck and the mother moaned, not able to believe her eyes.

'Mother,' Dr Daudi beckoned, 'come, wrap a blanket round him. He must be kept warm.'

For a moment she stood there dazed, then realising what had happened she wrenched the blanket from her shoulders, wrapped it round the child and held him close.

Baruti's cheerful voice called to the people. 'You saw this with your own eyes. You thought he was dead, drowned. We drained out the water and breathed into him until he was able to do it for himself.'

The mother looked up. 'You speak words of truth. My child breathes. He lives!'

Baruti beamed at her. 'Behold, it was only a little water that was in the child's lungs, but if it had stayed there it would have killed him. Behold, it doesn't take much sin to spoil the life that we live here on earth and to ruin the life that comes after it.'

'What life is that? What are these words?' demanded the man with the knobbed stick.

'It's the one that we shall live after we have no more use for our bodies,' said Baruti. 'The words are these: It is only Jesus, the Son of God, who can give us this life by taking the sin from deep within us.'

While Baruti answered questions and the crowd gradually dispersed, Yakobo stood shivering in the early morning sun.

'Take this,' cried Mboga. He dragged off his pullover and pulled it over Yakobo's head.

'Not big enough, Mboga,' laughed Tembo running to the Land Rover and bringing back the ground sheet.

As they walked slowly back to the Land Rover,

Yakobo spoke softly, 'It is good that the child lives again.'

Dr Matama smiled. 'The thing for him to remember is not to play on the slippery edges of swamps.'

The old twinkle was back in Yakobo's eye. 'Bwana, the matter is understood. I, too, have been in many dangerous places and have slipped hard and often. It seemed to me only this morning that my soul was sick to death and there was no hope. But as we worked on the boy, I asked Jesus to forgive me.'

'And you believe he will do so, Yakobo?'

'He has, yes. He has.'

The doctor smiled at Yakobo. 'We are going to work at Kitunda hospital for five days and there's nothing we'd like better than for you to come. You might care to lend a hand. We shall be more than busy.'

Yakobo was silent. The doctor pushed him into the Land Rover. 'Come on! The A.C. insists that you go before the court when we return to Mabwe.'

Yakobo nodded. 'But even in jail there will be opportunities.'

When they reached the hospital Yakobo borrowed a shirt and shorts, but he was ill at ease as the others walked to the operating theatre.

Dr Daudi put his hand on his shoulder. 'I'd like you to assist me with this operation.'

As Yakobo walked across to scrub his hands he caught a glimpse of the charm round his neck. He drew in his breath sharply. 'May I borrow scissors to cut this off?'

Daudi smiled and nodded. 'And you can put it in the bucket with the other rubbish.'

In the cool of the evening as they walked from the ward where their patients were doing well, Yakobo said, 'Bwana Daudi, do you think it is possible that later on there will still be work for me in the hospital?'

'If you want to travel God's way with all your heart and use your knowledge and your skill to help people to understand about him, yes, we want you, Yakobo. However, you would lose five years' seniority.'

Yakobo hesitated. 'But what of the things I stole?'

'You owe us twelve hundred shillings,' said Daudi slowly.

A look of dismay came over Yakobo's face. 'I had that sum many times over but it's all gone. How can I pay?'

His face grew longer. 'Also, I owe many people much money. I shall surely find myself in prison.'

'There is little doubt about the prison part,' agreed Daudi. 'But if you watch your spending you will be able to pay back your debts.'

Yakobo nodded. 'I can pay back half my wages every month.'

Six days later they left Kitunda hospital and stopped at the top of the pass that wound down the side of the Great Rift Wall. Baruti looked out over the Malenga country.

'Behold, it looks different. Much of the water has gone.'

'Let's get close and see,' urged Tembo.

Sixteen kilometres further on as the swamp came into view he wrinkled his nose. 'How that mud stinks!'

'Samuel Mkono is wasting no time,' grinned Baruti. 'That drumming noise must be the largest of his pumps.'

As they came closer they saw Pili Pili pointing to the edge of the swamp. In less than a minute they were all peering into a patch of churned-up sticky black mud.

Pili Pili was very excited. 'The animals come here to drink. They have to walk through that slush...'

'Down there!' yelled Tembo. 'See it?'

Four metres from the bank was something that struggled convulsively and produced loud continuous bellowing noises.

'It's a buffalo calf,' shouted Baruti.

'Punda's neck is not long enough to reach that unfortunate beast,' said Pili Pili. 'The nearer she came the deeper it went into the foul mud.'

Baruti had a rope. 'Will Punda hold me while I drop this over its neck?'

Pili Pili nodded and lowered the scoop end of his machine. Baruti scrambled in. A careful movement of levers and he was poised above the mud. Clutching with one hand and working the rope with the other he succeeded in dropping a loop right over the mud-spattered head.

Pili Pili was enjoying himself hugely. 'Punda has just suggested that if you pull too hard on that rope you will choke him and then he will be valuable only for food.'

Baruti took no notice. He was pulling as hard as he dared. Slowly more and more of the buffalo calf came into view. Abruptly the bellowing ceased. Mud had covered its eyes and ears and was clogging its mouth. Another rope was looped behind the back legs and soon buffalo was on the bank, so caked with mud that he was completely unable to move.

Baruti poured water into its mouth. This produced a couple of half-hearted bellows and then the small buffalo lay panting on the ground.

'Poor little beast,' said Baruti. 'We'll soon make things different for you.'

He and Tembo scraped the mud from its legs and beamed with satisfaction as it staggered to its feet. Without the slightest warning it charged Dr Daudi. He tripped, slid, and fell on his back in the slime.

'Listen to me, Buffalo,' said Baruti severely. 'That doesn't show much gratitude. We've just saved your life.'

Daudi was on his feet again, his neat white clothing a complete mess.

Pili Pili had difficulty keeping his face straight.

But Yakobo smiled at the doctor. 'Message understood.' He turned to all his friends. 'In future and with your help I shall be most careful not to follow the small wisdom of buffaloes.'

SAMPLE CHAPTER FROM:
JUNGLE DOCTOR'S
ENEMIES

1
A Rumour and a Blind Boy

Daudi and I walked through the hospital's hyaena-proof gate. Coming towards us was an African boy. He stumbled and nearly fell, clutching at the cornstalks growing on each side of the winding path. He steadied himself for a moment, then walked uncertainly forward.

I sprang towards him, 'What's the matter? Can I help?'

For a moment he stood silent and then exclaimed in a voice thick from crying, 'Bwana, the others will not let me help push the car because I am Mubofu, the blind one, and…' He turned and began to shuffle back the way he had come, his shoulders drooping and his hands groping in front of him.

Daudi put down the baskets of medicines and instruments he was carrying. 'Bwana, let's take him with us to Dodoma. It would bring him considerable joy.'

I nodded in agreement. As the boy turned towards us, I glimpsed at his face. It bore the stamp of tragedy. Two empty eye sockets told the story of hopeless native medicine. He clutched my arm. 'Bwana, I can push, even though I live in *utitu* – the land of darkness.'

'But what if you trip over as the car moves downhill?'

'*Kah*, Bwana, I am no stranger to falling. I have no fear of a bruise. Will you not allow me to help?'

The path curved round the trunk of a huge baobab tree. He unerringly followed the centre of the track to where Samson, the hospital handyman, was cranking on an A-model Ford. A group of small boys danced up and down and chanted, '*Na vilungo gwe, na vilungo* – go to it with strength!'

Samson straightened up and wiped his brow. '*Hongo*, Bwana, the battery is sleeping.'

I grinned. 'The row these *wadodo* – little people – are making should wake it, surely.'

'*Kah*, our car is not called Sukuma for nothing.' (*Sukuma* is the Swahili word for push.)

'Bwana, we'll push,' shouted the small boys, rushing forward.

'*Viswanu* – right – but you must wait for a moment till Daudi and I are ready.'

Changing from Chigogo, the language of the Central Plains of Tanzania, to English I said, 'Samson, we'll take that blind boy to Dodoma. Daudi and I think it would be a red-letter day in his life to go on safari with us. You can bring him back later on when we've caught the train.'

My African friend's reply was thoughtful. 'We can be eyes for him today and tell him all we see along the road and in the town.'

Mubofu was crouching in the shade of the mud-brick shed that was Sukuma's home. On the wall above him were three many-coloured lizards busily hunting flies. As I walked over to him he rose to his feet.

'Bwana, you'll let me help push?'

'How did you know it was I coming towards you?'

'*Hongo.*' His whole face lit up, his smile accentuating the hollows where his eyes should have been. '*Kah*, Bwana, I heard your shoes in the sand and I know no African who walks like you do.'

I whistled. 'What ears you've got!'

'Bwana, my ears have to be my eyes as well.' He put his hand on my sleeve. 'Bwana, please will you let me push?'

'No, Mubofu, I will not allow you to push.'

All the joy left his face. Before he could speak I said, 'But I wondered if perhaps you would like to come on safari with us today to Dodoma.'

'*Kah*,' exclaimed the boy, 'in the car, in Sukuma?'

'*Heya* – yes.'

'*Yoh*, Bwana, it has been my strong wish for many days to travel in a car. *Kah*!'

He proceeded to do a little dance which sent the lizards clambering up the trunk of the baobab tree. I went to collect my luggage and say my goodbyes.

As we walked back to the car I questioned Daudi. 'Tell me about Mubofu. What is his story?'

'His people are dead. He sleeps in the tribal house of his relations in a village which has no time for the ways of God. I have heard it said that they feed him only because they think he will die before long anyhow, and it is a thing of small wisdom to upset the spirits of the ancestors.'

Mubofu was running his fingers over the radiator and bonnet of the car. We wedged him into the front seat between Samson and Daudi. Letting off the hand-brake I called out, '*Alu sukuma* – come on, push!'

Slowly we moved forward under twenty-boy power. The old machine gained speed as we rolled down the stony track from the hospital. I let in the clutch. Sukuma backfired noisily. Shrieking, the children scampered away. Then the engine started and we were on the first lap of a medical safari to the top of the Great Rift Wall.

We moved cautiously down a crazily cut track running through a dry river bed.

Mubofu spoke excitedly, 'It's on the hill beyond the fourth river that I live. Do I not know this part of the road very well indeed?'

'Truly,' said Daudi, 'he travels this road as well as anybody. His feet seem to know every rock and rut.'

'It was here, Bwana, at Chibaya, that I was born. It was here that I lost my eyes.'

'How did it happen, Mubofu?'

The blind boy held up four fingers. 'It was four years ago, Bwana, when *serenyenyi* came into our village.'

I looked at Daudi. His lips framed the word measles.

'*Hongo*,' continued Mubofu, 'those were days of sorrow, Bwana. First my nose and then my eyes ran. Ehh, how I coughed! My *wandugu* – relations – would not let me sleep. They beat tins and shouted and shook me. "You must not sleep or you'll die," they said. Then, Bwana, my eyes became filled with pain because of the glare and the flies. When they put me inside the house the smoke of the cooking fires made my eyes worse still.'

He sat up suddenly and pointed with his chin towards a group of huts. 'There is my house. There, Bwana, is where it all happened.'

'*Kah*,' said Samson, 'how do you know we've come to your house?'

'*Kumbe*,' explained the boy, 'is my nose not awake? Shall I not know the smell of my own village?'

There was silence for a while and then he said, 'Bwana, there was pain, fiery pain. In my eyes were ulcers. But there was no one to help me.'

Something was moving in the jungle beside the road. Samson shouted, 'Look, Bwana, *mpala*...' A buck the size of a Shetland pony sprang up from a thornbush thicket and bounded away in great leaps.

'What was it?' asked Mubofu, his hand on my shoulder.

'A beautiful buck. See, there behind it is another.'

As the words passed my lips I tried to stop them from slipping out, but the boy's face was aglow. 'I can see it, Bwana, in my mind. *Yoh*, how they jump.'

The road wound in and out through thornbush country. My thoughts were about measles, remembering that worldwide epidemics occurred every five years. Another was due shortly if the wretched disease came on schedule.

We crossed a dry riverbed which in the wet season could be a muddy torrent. 'Daudi, we must be prepared for another measles epidemic and not let this sort of thing happen again.'

Daudi nodded, 'They don't only go blind when measles attacks. Hundreds and hundreds of children die. Behold, in our own country it is a disease of trouble and death and sorrow, especially for children.'

I looked at the pitiful face beside me and thought of the torment that small boy must have suffered. He, however, was not thinking of measles and was tense with excitement. Each stage of that journey had its own particular interest to him. He amazed me as time and again he described what we had passed. His senses were unusually quick. He sat there alert as Sukuma sputtered and skidded along the Great North Road.

We were climbing a steep hill on which cactus flourished. Immediately below was a patch of dark green mango trees growing round the sandy riverbed; amongst them were the white buildings of a large boys' school. We turned off the road and drove through a peanut garden and past a carpentry workshop where schoolboys were busy making tables.

I stopped the car in the shade of a great kikuyu tree. 'It's time for food. Later we'll drive to the railway station.'

I heard from my friend, the principal of the school, that a measles epidemic had actually started. It was way up in the north in the Sudan and Kenya. 'There's no news of it in Tanzania – yet.'

The station-master, a tall Indian, informed me that the train was six hours late. He told me of a severe epidemic in his home town, Hyderabad. It sounded suspiciously like measles to me.

Samson was pumping up Sukuma's tyres. He looked up enquiringly as I came through the station gate.

'The train is six hours late,' I told them.

Mubofu laughed. '*Hongo*, Bwana, that is good. Behold, you will have time to tell me many things about Dodoma. I will see in my mind what you see with your eyes. I have never been in a place where there were so many people.'

Jungle Doctor Series

Jungle Doctor and the Whirlwind
ISBN 978-1-84550-296-6

Jungle Doctor on the Hop
ISBN 978-1-84550-297-3

Jungle Doctor Spots a Leopard
ISBN 978-1-84550-301-7

Jungle Doctor's Crooked Dealings
ISBN 978-1-84550-299-7

Jungle Doctor's Enemies
ISBN 978-1-84550-300-0

CHRISTIAN FOCUS PUBLICATIONS

Christian   Christian   CF4K   Mentor
Focus   Heritage

Christian Focus Publications publishes books for adults and children under its four main imprints: Christian Focus, CF4K, Mentor and Christian Heritage. Our books reflect that God's word is reliable and Jesus is the way to know him, and live for ever with him.

Our children's publication list includes a Sunday School curriculum that covers pre-school to early teens; puzzle and activity books. We also publish personal and family devotional titles, biographies and inspirational stories that children will love.

If you are looking for quality Bible teaching for children then we have an excellent range of Bible story and age specific theological books.

From pre-school to teenage fiction, we have it covered!

Find us at our web page:
www.christianfocus.com

CF4•K
Because you're never too young to know Jesus